ere, with sweet champagne pulsing tl

On my boy becoming a man

Rain's Great

—The First and Last Gift

"Wind sweeping now over my bare back."

To Make a Marriage Live or Die

When You're Twelve Years Old,
Then Read This

, my Little Ones?

Listen to Your Pappy's Music

Starting the Day

and beautiful Christmas…

Nothing of Money

he Church of Earth and Sky

When You're Eighteen, Do Not Read

The Losing of Love

efore"

of What's Important in Life

"I have some things
I want to leave you both."

Travel the World

Birthing and Raising Kids

"Thank You" and "Please"

Your Pappy's Love of Books and
All Appearances of the Mother Tongue

Growing Old

Take A Walk

appy Number Ten!!!

"I give to you our vows… Our wedding vows."

The Legacy Letters

Lucas

Enilot a great pleasure to meet you at the ALA!

Best regards, [signature]

June 2016

Early Evening —

It looks like a few rain clouds are trying
to break through the mountain tops. I can see the edge,
and beyond that... Mt. something rises over the small
black fuzzy cloud. Grandpa points to the peaks
and Kevin raises to sharpen, often will remember a
ridge. He looks amused. Loves to listen to it.
Long to sing it. Kevin it dozes to it. He wants his
say. He finds it like Grandpa has switched on the
if you don't follow any better, again think e Kevin
dozes easier if Kevin were around very fit.
Mostly just took him on. Grandpa suggests
happier that super to any breathing music, being
Grandma after summer feature, or washing a few
cook just starting to walk.

The
Legacy Letters

his wife, his children,
his final gift

Written by
CAREW PAPRITZ

The Legacy Letters
Copyright © 2013 by Carew Papritz

*Inspired, Created, Written, Edited, Designed, Printed, and
Made in the United States of America*

ISBN: 978-0-9857088-7-0
Library of Congress Control Number: 2012909888

The Legacy Letters™ is a trademark of King Northern, Inc.
King Northern™ is a trademark of King Northern, Inc.

*Cover design by Don Faia
Interior design by Alan Hebel of the Book Designers
All imagery courtesy of the author, with the exception
of various illustrations by Rawhide Papritz and
cover images by RM Tremayne*

The Legacy Letters is available for special promotions and premiums.
For details, contact sales@KingNorthern.com

King Northern
PUBLISHING

www.TheLegacyLetters.com

"What alluring brightness glimmers within the beribboned package?"
First Edition

Night of our night...

Listen to your Fingers Music

Begins, Little One,

As listening to the Victrola again. It's
night, and the piano echoes of a pian-
ist came ringing, as though this year was
before me. You imagine his massive black silhou-
ette... gave yellow light of the lantern, running g
morning as he curves up the smoke music
slips away. Chopin begins to play q the cabin
glistening gets winding their way through the
floating up and against the magic journey,
He may journeys of wind and rain, ring
you journeyment of going time.

My god! Little One, how I love...

December 23—

Mr. Tremayne—Editor
8806 Cutterson Street
Seattle, WA 98002

Dear Mr. Tremayne—Editor:

I T WAS NINETEEN years ago that my husband and I faced what seemed an irreconcilable difference, now minor in retrospect, that caused us to separate. Shortly after his leaving, I found that I was pregnant with twins, but out of anger I did not share this information with him. It was at this time that our tragedy deepened. My husband learned that he was terminally ill and then heard through a mutual friend that I was pregnant. For fear of placing my pregnancy in jeopardy, he decided not to notify me of his impending death. Instead, he lived alone for another seven months, dying far away from his family and friends.

On the tenth birthday of our children, they received from their father, through his former attorney, the enclosed set of letters. It furnished for them the essential memory of their father that I had been unable to provide. His words not only consoled them but exerted a powerful and welcome influence upon their personal lives. The revelation of my husband's noble spirit, and his expressed feelings of love and remorse, also paved the way for my forgiveness.

My husband was a man with whom I had begun to share an extraordinary relationship before he, I, and fate joined forces to end it. Despite my own continuing feelings of personal loss, grief, and remorse, I have agreed with my son and daughter's decision to offer these letters for publication. In doing so, we wish not only to honor my husband's and their father's memory, but to share with others the unique message with which he comforted and inspired us.

Yours respectfully,
(Name Withheld as Requested)

From R. M. Tremayne
Editor of *The Legacy Letters*

"How These Letters Came to Be"

Dear Reader,

THE LETTERS THAT compose this volume came into my hands, as editor, under unusual circumstances. A personal note from the widow, found on the previous page and which I have been given permission to quote, accompanied the photocopied letters. Our firm was allowed to publish the letters but with three stipulations: the author was to remain anonymous, his biographical material was to be brief, and any possibly ensuing profits from publication were to be donated to a stated charity.

The author of these astonishing letters was formerly the editor and publisher of a small-town newspaper but, drawn back by tradition, he sold this business and returned to running his family's cattle ranch. An individualist by nature, he enjoyed the solitary pursuits of flying and mountain climbing. As an avocation, he prospected informally for silver, gold, and semi-precious stones. Yet he was also sociable, played the piano and guitar, and often entertained his wife and friends with songs he had written. Left to his children, along with his letters and echoing their message in spirit, were the music and lyrics of his last songs.

After the succession of beginning events described by his wife in her letter, the author retreated to a remote wilderness valley close to his birthplace and attempted no further personal communication. Previous to his self-exile, however, he mailed to his attorney a letter that he requested be opened in the late spring of the following year. Upon broaching this letter, the lawyer discovered, to his sincere dismay, that his young rancher friend and client had died.

The letter included a series of unusual requests. The attorney was asked to travel to a cabin remotely located in a mountainous region of an adjacent state, there to secure a set of letters the client had left to his children. The rancher's wife was not to be informed of the death of her husband because he himself wished to notify her in a special letter. Knowledge of the existence of the bequeathed letters was to be withheld from her also. Finally, the lawyer was to assure delivery of the gift of letters to the author's children in a decade's time.

The attorney executed all of his client's requests faithfully. Shortly after the spring snow melt, he succeeded in bringing out by packhorse the packet of letters, a small trunk containing some personal effects, and the special letter the author had addressed to his wife. In later years, commenting upon his experience, the attorney would tell of his first sighting of the metal box, sitting fatefully on the rustic wooden table. Upon unlocking the small chest, he had observed in awe the large bundle of intimate letters within, carefully double-wrapped, first in leather rawhide and then in canvas oil skin. And he would continue to relate that as he exited from the cabin carrying the author's legacy, a squirrel had jumped from the building's shingle roof onto the metal box, paused there as if to reclaim it, then leaped to the ground to disappear into the surrounding forest.

The author's wife, undergoing now the responsibility of raising the twins alone, was feeling an increased anger about her husband's assumed abandonment and failure to communicate. At this stressful juncture she received his delayed letter. From it she learned not only that he was dead but that he had died four months previously in a state of dire loneliness. Becoming grief-stricken at the news, she required for some time the help of close relatives and friends in the daily management of the ranch.

Added to the pain of her husband's death was the shock of his choice of death site. After experiencing in this, his thirty-third year, some of the most significant events of his life, both joyful and tragic, he had felt compelled to face even his day of death alone. He could not return home, he said, for the same reasons that he had stayed away. He did not wish to die inside a lonely cabin. It was pointless to summon human aid, only to die within the confines of a hospital. Since both of them were mountain climbers, he knew that she would understand his choosing to retreat to the heights. He had selected the small cave located up valley from the cabin, in the north face of the peak they both had climbed some time ago.

By early fall of that year, before first snow, the wife was able to assemble a group of climbing friends to help her in bringing down the body of her husband from the mountain. Explaining her decision, she said, "I don't want him to remain up there alone forever. I know that he would want to be brought home." Her hopes were soon granted, and in a small private ceremony conducted at sunset, she was able to inter her beloved, and her estranged, in the all-forgiving soil of the ranch's ancestral cemetery.

The wife had been the first to enter the cliffside cave. There she found the body of her husband, still well preserved by the cold. Having transcended his pale of suffering, he seemed almost serene. The required autopsy that followed, though recognizing the ravaging effects of fatal disease, pronounced the immediate cause of death to have been hypothermia.

Positioned beside the body of the author was a wooden box, made of rough-hewn juniper, that contained an array of personal possessions: a handful of ranch dirt in a deerskin pouch, a worn leather bridle, several well used pipes, letters from his wife and various close friends, an assortment of photographs and sketches, and a few small samples of ore-bearing rocks. Tucked inside his shirt was a woven cotton foldover safeguarding a lock of his wife's hair. In his right fist, still tightly grasped, the deceased held a sprig of fragrant sage.

Secured elsewhere, for safe delivery in a full decade, were the author's carefully handwritten letters in which he had attempted to distill into words the multiple essences of human existence as he perceived them. These personal revelations he would convey through time, to the wife with whom he longed to reunite, and to the children he would never physically see but whom he wished to touch with a special, spiritual intimacy.

In my close reading of *The Legacy Letters*, as I readied the manuscript for publication, I found myself unusually moved by the author's honest reach for truth; his infinite passion, both exultant and despairing; his imagistic skill; his rhythmical sense, timed to some mysterious source, perhaps Shakespearean meter or the human heartbeat; and, in general, the broad range of his style and tone. Even his entries of day and night emerge as starkly different in their feeling, the former tending toward assurance and objectivity, the latter toward doubt and subjective haunting.

My ultimate reflection upon *The Legacy Letters* is that it is more than just an exceptional declaration of a deep devotion to children and of an unending love for a woman. It is, in the final analysis, a universal poetic testament, metaphysical in nature, to one individual's fervent and abiding faith in life, love, mankind, nature, and a Supreme Power that he felt was guiding worlds without end in unjudgeable omniscience.

R.M. Tremayne

R.M. Tremayne

Editor

From Our Family to You…

O UT OF THE more than two hundred letters written by our father, our family eventually chose over forty for the publication of this particular book. Our most difficult task was deciding not only which letters to leave in, but which to take out, for many are wise as others are magical, many enlightening as others are haunting.

Throughout the years, these life letters, love letters, and spiritual letters have instructed us, inspired us, and even helped define us. Many have become family favorites. Others are personally intimate. Some are magnificent. And all are truly revealing. His words, much like the songs he also left to us, are soulful, curious, provocative, tragic, passionate, and timeless.

Through these letters, a man discovered his life. In these letters, we found our father. His final gift, to our mother and to us, changed our lives forever. Yet we know this gift cannot end with us. Now this gift must be given to you, the reader, to find your own wisdom, inspiration, and hope within these Legacy Letters—and hopefully and somehow to be changed forever.

July 6
4:49 A.M.
39 degrees.

Good Morning, Future Chess,

To open my eyes, look out the window, go
see (my) painting the top of forever ... in for sure
to feel my leg still gripped in my ... from ...
I fell asleep last night. still can't ... you
... awoke with this is the first thought of the ...
Now that's bitter sweet.

I'm not who you are, but what you're most
it's not where you come from, but where you ...
so much yet to be learned.

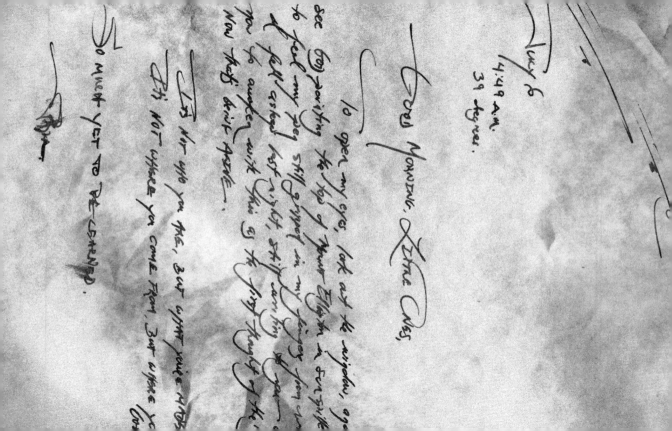

The
Legacy Letters

3:42 in the afternoon
Northbound on a Great Northern train

To My Son and Daughter,

I AM WRITING THESE WORDS to you on the leeward end of my last train ride north. Moving and clicking away on these lullaby tracks... If my scrawl looks a bit like I'm writing with frostbitten fingers in the middle of some Antarctic white-out, then ask your mom to decipher. How she was able to read all my coffee-stained and snow-smeared letters over the years is beyond me.

Looks like a summer squall off toward the northwest. Black rain against a prairie-blue sky. We'll be tunneling into it pretty soon.

I can't quite imagine how we are meeting now. With you both opening this strange box on the kitchen table. There still must be snow on the ground, and the old Majestic cookstove must be all fired up, good pine heat warming up the morning. So curious you must be. Like little calves poking their heads through the fence with big eyes and a headful of curiosity. The day after your tenth birthday. Maybe there's cake still under the glass and balloons bobbing down from the rafters. I imagine your mom sitting next to you in the big wicker chair next to the window. That was always her throne. A big cup of coffee at her ready.

Maybe she is reading this letter to you now. Or maybe she is listening to you read it out loud. And now, from an old metal payroll box, you pull out a big stack of letters tied up with thin strips of old harness leather. These letters before you—hopefully not too yellowed. Later you'll open a wooden trunk full of old knickknacks, keepsakes, and relics—junkeries, crumbs, and leavings of your old man's life that might make you wonder about who he really was and why he left you these things. Some music I've written. A couple of old love poems to your mom. An old flag that I carried with me for years. This is what I imagine I will be giving to you. For I have not yet written the letters, nor filled the box with memories, nor finished the music for your ears, nor given you any poems. This is what I plan to do. Such a strange cheat of time— to no longer exist even as you read me now. Like bending gravity just to get to you.

How do you say hello to your son and daughter whom you've never met. Will never meet. What do you say. How do you explain. How do you begin?

We might as well start out with honesty. I've always found it a good place to begin. I'm dying. I wish I could say it was otherwise, but I can't. I wish I could say it a little less bluntly, but I can't do that either.

I've been given a handful of months to put my house in order. In one respect I'm lucky. My life won't pass before my eyes—it <u>is</u> before my eyes. My "now" exists in a short but definite space of time so that I'll have the chance to prepare for my extinction. No luckless auto accident or pre-ordained heart attack. No vegetable half-state with ungodly plastic tubes worming their way out of my body. No war-gutting wound. No silly cosmic "oops you missed a turn—you lose." No, sir. Just a straightfor-ward, get-on- with-it, good old-fashioned death.

I'm also fortunate (maybe not the best choice of words) because I'm going to be forced to think about and sum up my total existence. Not something you would normally take on as a hobby. More like hard labor. Like digging postholes in the back forty in that damnable hardpan of fused red rock and soil. You do it one posthole at a time. Hands blistered. Metal hitting rock, striking back at bone. And you keep on going because that's what you have to do. It's my job now to understand being alive.

My eyes are wide open now. I feel for the first time, fully awake. Able to make peace with my god or the gods. Smelling dusk, pine, horse and saddle for the last time. Choosing perhaps to throw myself into the insurrection of some late autumn thunderstorm. Enjoying possibly one last snowfall. Certainly dreaming of a final kiss from the woman I love. And that fine bottle of heathered Scotch, having waited twenty-eight years, will share in my ultimate gala.

To die and live at the same time—the oddest and most beautiful absurdity imaginable. Like being walked

Dusk—

I have to confess that I'm continuing this letter now
from a bar on the threadbare edge of the known universe
with refrains of Hank Williams and Merle Haggard croon-
ing into the darkest corners. The train left me off several
hours ago. In the rain, naturally. It's beating down on the
roof here like some irksome banshee that's got nothing
but time to waste for a living.

I'm drinking something I think is beer, but if it
is, it too is dying. The ever universal bar mirror looks at
me and I at it. From my crow's nest stool I can see the
many productive tax-payers who have conjoined for a
little early-evening fortitude. A scattering of cowmen and
truckers. A local drunk welded to the other end of the
bar. All making small talk, if that. I know these people.
We are alone without being alone. That is how this parlor
game of solitude and camaraderie is played. Respecting
each other's silent war with living.

Ahhhhh, damn it all, Patsy Cline just came on—
"Faded Love." Nothing like being tortured by the wrong
love song. (I'd better go feed the jukebox myself. Seven

songs for a buck. Not bad. If the deck is going to be stacked, I want it to be in my favor).

I would give up all the wishes of Aladdin to be with you and your mother at the moment of your arrival, but this isn't going to happen. So, from the standpoint of all that's pragmatic, I'm going to enter your lives on this your tenth birthday. I figure ten is a couple steps shy of becoming a man or a woman. I wish I could address you by your baptized names, but since that's not possible, I'll settle for a rose by any other name and call you Little Ones.

Dear Little Ones,

These letters are my birthday present to you both. I figure I'll make good use of my dying by writing you a manual of life according to your pa. My plan is to write you a little bit about everything I feel is worth knowing about living. A series of how-to and what-if letters. Since your old man has more opinions than there are flickers in a fire (as your mom well knows), I won't be shy with the paper. And maybe I can perform part of my fatherly duty by way of pen.

I'd also like to postpone my being recycled into the universal compost pile until I've said my piece to you both. I need to know that all I've experienced in life is not going to just disappear into the mountains once I'm gone. I suppose these letters then are also my stab at immortality. Actually, you're my immortality. But I need to give you something real of who I am. This paper and ink—and thoughts. Something you can touch, to know that I was once flesh and blood, a man and a father.

These letters—a horse trough of the practical, a smidgen of the idealistic, and a ladleful of whatever else I think might be useful.

If you're not sure which mares need to go to Cougar's pasture for the summer, I'll tell you. If you're buying a used truck and there's a clack when there should be click, I'll try to help you there—or send you to one of your uncles. I'll give you what I know about standing up to bullies or telling time by the North Star. If it's how to build a perfect snowball, cure a bad cold, find true love, pick out a good cigar, write a poem, or climb a mountain... well, you get the picture—I'll be there.

I wish there had been a "manual" like this when I was growing up. Something besides the Good Book and the Boy Scout handbook, you understand. Something a little more day-by-day functional. Giving me the nuts and bolts of it all. But being a kid, I probably wouldn't have paid a silver heck to it anyhow but gone on being as bull-stubborn as ever, trying to figure out life in my own pasture. That's the job of being a kid.

More than likely you'll do well enough alone by the engines of your own fate until you either hit a few really nasty bumps in the road or grow old enough to realize that there may be a diamond or two in what you thought was your old man's coal bucket.

(Here comes "Somewhere over the Rainbow." Know that your pa is an incurable romantic, but I figure it's the only sickness worth having. Ever since I was a kid I've always gone just short of bawling whenever I heard Miss Garland sing this song, Incurable…)

It's time to leave this last refuge of civility and merry-makery and move on to higher pastures. I toast you both. It's a harsh and spectacular world that awaits you. Know that I love you.

Your Pa.

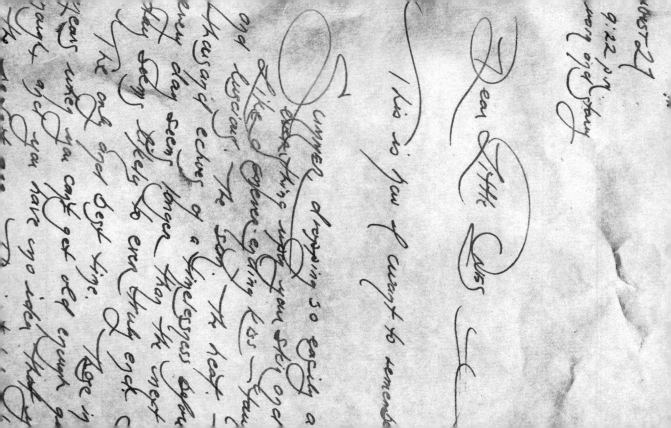

AUGUST 21
9:22 p.m.
more open sky

Dear Little Luis

I kiss you I want to remember

SUMMER is running so easily a
everything ... you ... her
like a opening kiss ... shy ...
and luscious. The sun. The heat
thousand echoes of a timelessness before
every day seem longer than the next
they seem likely to ever think of.
The only ... get best time. ... Age is
years ... you can't get old enough a
... you have go into think ...

Summer...

July 2—

Dear Little Ones,

Congratulations and Happy Number Ten!!!

Ten years on this planet. Time to whoop it up like Indians. Jump over fences. Cause a conniption and a bucketful of mischief. Dance a monkey-doodle. Just don't break any windows or scare the horses. Put on the dog and kick out the cats. It's time to celebrate your first double-digit adventure into adulthood.

And here's your birthday present as I promised, though still invisible to my naked eye (because officially it hasn't been started yet)—it will, subject to the magical and somewhat hurly-burlish beater bowl of time/space and God's grace, hopefully arrive fully completed as one bonafide manual-of-life.

I am sure that if you've received these letters-to-be then you'll also have received a box of mementos: photos of your mom and me climbing in the mountains, rock samples from various mining forays, a smattering of sentimental jibs and jangles, and a small book of poems I wrote years ago. You should also have in your possession my guitar— "Cherokee" (all guitars should have a name), a bottle of Jim Beam passed on to me when I was a kid by old Tanner Daws, who cowboyed on the ranch for years, a French champagne I picked up in Norway, and my old Hamley saddle which your grandpa gave me. Most of these relics I've already prepared to send to you.

I've tossed in a sheaf of lyrics and a few cassette tapes of songs I've written over the years. Was a time I entertained the idea of actually making a living from music, rather than playing for just drinks or kisses. I thought you might want to know how hot or not your pop was on the old six-string. By the time you receive the songs they might be considered old-fashioned. Such are the conniption moods of time. I've also decided to write you a few songs to go along with the letters—to serve you up a full course rather than just a soup and salad. Never was one for halfway of a bare minimum.

I know your mom won't mind the champagne. It's her favorite. I know she always enjoyed a good glass of giggle and a celebration in the name of most anything. A tenth birthday is as good enough reason as any to begin learning about the finer rarities of living. So take a big sip!

I hope that these letters-to-be and music-to-be-made will help you to see your old man as more than just a stack of pictures or the butt of a few crazy stories from your uncles. I've lived a little and loved a bit more. I've also thought much about you both.

So, crank up the music, pop the champagne, sit back, and get to know your old man. He'd sure like to get to know you. Give my love to your Mother.

Happy Birthday, Little Ones!!!

Your Pa.

Night
Quiet and clear

Dear Little Ones,

A FTER A FINE ALL-PURPOSE DAY of traipsing through the aspens and sage, repairing the cabin walls, chatting with the local mountains, and fishing for my supper, I think it's time to sit down with my pen, my head, and this quiet night, and try to write down what I believe to be the essentials of life—your pa's pocket commandments—something you can keep tucked in your trouser pockets as a sort of life map. To keep you on track or out of trouble. Like a pocketknife—it's always there.

I've never been down this road before but I figure if Moses could do it then maybe he's onto something. I hope someday you'll do the same with your own life—with your own kids. After lying under the stars for a spell, here's what I came up with:

Your Old Man's Declaration of What's Important in Life

   Your good health.
   Your good name.
   Your true happiness.
   Keeping a compassionate heart and a tolerant mind.

Believing deeply in whatever you believe in.
Standing by each other—your mom, your family,
and friends, no matter what.
Laughing as much as possible, whenever possible.

Fight when you have to.
Know when you are humbled.
Live honorably, and with manners and grace.
Stay curious, dream often—to keep your spirit alive.
Be generous with your life—love deeply, honestly,
and without reservation.
Know when and how to forgive.
Take care of your land and your animals.
Keep your word.

And here's all the rest of what I believe and know...

Please Say "Thank You" and "Please"

Dear Little Ones,

I'VE SEEN MY FAIR SHARE of spoiled brats and rude donkey knobs, and I'm here to tell you that above all else it is preferable to carry the true grace of being a lady or a gentleman with you for the rest of your life rather than succumb to the pig-inspired manners of sassy-mouthed jerks and other irrelevant pieces of human wreckage.

This world is going to hell in a handbasket. Civility seems like some nasty throwback to the days of tipping your hat to, and opening a door for, a woman. If we, as aspiring animals do nothing else, we should attain to the most refined elements of our accreted civilization. We should be polite. Being polite is nothing more than dignity personified as action. It is the mettle of our animalhood. It is the refinement of our dignity through his ability to be polite. If you only pretend to be polite, you are a resourceful hypocrite who should do just fine in our apish world of skullduggery and idiocy, and more than likely you will be admitted to the gates of whatever middle hell welcomes such people. Politeness must carry the true weight of sincerity and integrity for it to be a true act of politeness.

As your parental watchbird, I would ask you to be highly mindful of the fact that being polite is not only good human politics, it is also good humanity.

So:

Say "Thank you."

Say "Please."

Apologize sincerely.

Open doors for people.

Say "Excuse me" when appropriate.

Say "Ma'am" or "Sir" when appropriate.

And, in general, be a nice person. It works.

—Your Pa

When You're Twelve Years Old, Then Read This

Dear Little Ones,

TWELVE. THE PERFECT AGE. Naïve enough to still be curious—and innocent. Young enough to get yourself in trouble without knowing how to get out of it. And old enough to have acquired the necessary insight into the subtle and not-so-subtle kid politics of the-carrot-and-the-stick dance.

Twelve. When school hours are five times as long as summer hours. When getting hugged by your mom or pop is still okay. When getting tucked into bed is still a necessity. When it's still a hassle to take a bath. When eating asparagus and Brussels sprouts are still worse than going to prison. When marbles and dogs are still more exciting than girls, and when horses and girlfriends are still more exciting than boys.

If you both could see me now. All grin and memory. To be twelve and never know how perfect life really is at that one moment in time— Okay, enough reminiscing. You still have to tap the tune at twelve. It's not all cotton-candy and rainbow endings. So here are a few tricks of the twelve-year-old trade that might just nudge you closer to obtaining childhood nirvana (if you're not already there), or help keep you there (if you already are).

Chores—Do your chores, then go out and play.

Homework—Do your homework, then go out and play.

Learn to play a musical instrument, but only if you enjoy it. Your mom can play a mean flute and your grandma kicks out a choice "Night and Day" on the piano. Decide which songs you like and then learn how to play them. Playing music shouldn't be boring or stupid.

Everyone has nightmares. It's okay to have them. But whenever you're caught in the grips of some scary hobgoblin, go to your brother or sister or mother and tell them about it. Of course, the best part of having a nightmare is being able to crawl under someone's covers, cuddle up next to them, and fall back to sleep.

Get someone—anyone—to read books to you. Having books read to you at any age is the supremo ultimato of living.

Read what you like, not what you're told to like. That way you'll read for a lifetime.

Learn to cook. Your mom is a great cook. She'll teach you. Cooking is not nuclear physics. It's cooking. Read the directions, listen to your mom, and always offer your sister or your brother a fair chance to scrape out the cake bowl.

Don't mumble. Find your voice and have your say. Mumbling is for a mouth full of cookies or for when you're speaking at a mumblers convention.

Life isn't always fair—when you're a kid. You'll have figured this out by now, so I'm not telling you anything new. Just realize that being a kid and being treated fairly don't always go together. You can't always get what you want, and you don't get to vote on it either. That's because your parents are benevolent dictators. They think they know what's best for you, and generally they do. Not always, but mostly. When you grow up to be a parent, you'll know what I mean.

Play sports. Even if it's just to try them out, to see if you like them.

Don't talk back to your mom—talk with her.

Respect those folks who deserve respecting. Usually they'll be older than you.

Don't say mean or nasty things to anyone.

Be kind to all animals.

Learn to listen. Then you'll learn when to speak.

Don't whine. Whining is whining at any age, whoever does it. Just don't do it.

If you can't eat what's on your plate, try to sneak it to the dogs. This is not what a grownup is supposed to say. I know this. But everyone has pulled this trick at some time or another in their lives. Otherwise, just say you can't eat everything and take the consequences.

Always protect your brother.

Always protect your sister.

And always look out for your family. Always.

Keep your eyes peeled when you cross any street or road. This is really important. Even when you're crossing the old Harshaw road. Because, unless you're looking down the road, then you're not looking. Which, of course, applies both to cars and life.

Do not talk to strangers or take anything from a stranger unless your mom or another grownup says it's okay.

Be as honest as a looking glass and tell the truth. It's just a good lifetime policy to follow…

Sometimes you may feel as if you just don't fit into this world. That happens. Stumble around then and be curious about all and anything your heart desires until you fall perfectly into your passions. Then throw yourself into them—and don't hesitate. Give your best to them. No halfways. Halfway is like riding a side saddle. Why do it? And don't listen to those who try to discourage you from making new starts in life. Life is all about exploring the new and untried. Finally, enjoy what you are learning and doing. This is one of the hardest concepts in the entire world to understand. Harder yet to put into practice.

Always close the gates so the cows don't get out.

Learn to say grace and mean it.

Share what you want to share and, if you don't want to, then say so.

If you have a question, ask it. Ask it with respect and honesty. If people don't give you a good answer, ask them again until they understand that you are serious about the question. If some jackass posing as an adult tells you he can't be bothered, be polite, kick him in the shins, and then run. And if you can't do that (because your Mom will hang me for even suggesting it), then just ignore the person altogether. As your grandpa would say, "They're about as useless as tits on a boar pig." And he's right.

If someone asks you a question and you don't know the answer, say, "I don't know." There's no disgrace in not knowing everything, just in pretending you do.

Help your mom when she asks you to.

Kick the mud off your boots before you walk into the kitchen.

Get to dinner on time.

I'm sure there are other important things that I should be telling you at the glorious age of twelve, but I can't think of them right now. It's a good age. Enjoy it while you're there.

In twelve-year-old reverie,

Papa

I T LOOKS LIKE A FEW rain clouds are trying to breed on the mountain tops. I can see Echo Ridge, and beyond that Mt. Satchmo towers over the small black, feudal clouds. Grandpa named the peaks around here however he wanted, often with music on his mind. He loved music. Loved to listen to it. Loved to sing it, hum it, dance to it. It made his face light up like someone had just switched on the sun. His body would go to twitching and, if you didn't know any better, you'd think a few angels inside of him were throwing glory fits. Music just took him over. Grandpa was never happier than when he was breathing music, seeing Grandma after summer pasture, or watching a newborn colt just starting to walk.

Right here where I stand, on the cabin's front porch, I can look up valley and see most of his Musical Mountains. Starting toward the east of the valley are the jazz peaks of Satchmo and Ellington. I can see Mount Beethoven and there's Haydn's Glacier coming off it. A little shy and to the west of the glacier is the opera arête of Madam Butterfly. And there, by the grace of god (as Grandpa would ever intone) is Mount Ava (as in Gardner, who wasn't musical but was musical in body). On a real clear day you can see Mount Bob Wills with all the smaller peaklets around being the Texas Playboys.

And of course, without a doubt, there is Mount Hank. A couple of the smaller peaks have odd names like Mount Champagne Strawberry and Mount Paris Perdu, and Mount Peek-a-Boo and Mount Hide-a-Horse. I figured they were just reminders of old memories, like of war buddies he wanted to remember or lost loves that might not really be lost. Or maybe he was just plain having fun. I guess if he wanted to tell me how he named them he would have.

Grandpa wasn't much for brag talk. When I asked him who named the peaks he told me they just named themselves and that he was the only one around who would listen to them sing. Since nobody ever came up to the high pasture except himself, he ordained himself as the unofficial name-giver for all the promontories and pinnacles for as far as he could see. As a kid, I sure as heck didn't know any better. Years later I was talking to some Forest Service fellow about the area and he had no idea what I was talking about. He showed me a map and there in official U.S.G.S. 9-point Roman type was a whole other world, named by God-knows-who, existing on official looking paper but as far as I was concerned not existing at all.

Grandpa built this cabin back when there were still a few Indians around. Seems like they were always hungry. They never stole a cow from him while he ran the cow camp. They'd always ask him and he'd give them some old heifer that had gone dry. He knew what made good humanity and good politics.

The Aermotor windmill he packed in here in 1912 is still working. I can still make out the faded streaks of red paint on the rudder that say it was made in Chicago. That's where he went to get the windmill, got shot at, and met Grandma. I'd pester Grandpa to death to tell me all about the wild days in Chi-caaah-go, and of course about the union battles of the miners in Idaho and Montana, and when he cowboyed in Texas and in Mexico where Pancho Villa was still riding over the border—and I could go on and on. I'd do anything to get him going on a story. Heck, that's what I lived for. Grandpa's stories. He didn't die a rich man but, as he would occasionally bluster to me, "He who dies with the best stories wins." By my reckoning Gramps was, I'm sure, a millionaire many times over.

The windmill sits on the backside of the beaver pond. I think the sucker rod is busted. I should fix it pretty soon. It's something Gramps would have wanted done yesterday and before breakfast.

Grandpa picked this spot so he'd always have a perfect view of the mountains. He was a king of a grand kingdom. Aligned his castle so that the summer sun would shine through the front window for as long as it stayed above the ridge line. This was his home on and off for just shy of twenty seasons. He made his money on a hunch. Had a small gold claim up in northern Washington. Made enough for him to buy the ranch and to head back up here during the summers. And here is where my teaching took place. And as history bites its own tail, this is where I'll try to pass on to you both a bit of what I've learned.

There are a few cow elk drinking at the north side of the lake. The rain is starting to fall off. I thought you two might want to know a few details about where I am, and how I once lived and am living now.

Time to take a look at that sucker rod. I'll talk to you both later on.

Love,
Your Pa

July 6

4:49 a.m.
39 degrees

Good Morning, Little Ones,

T O OPEN MY EYES, look out the window, and see God painting the top of Mount Ellington in sun-spilled gold—to feel my pen still gripped in my fingers from when I fell asleep last night, still writing to you—and now to awaken with this as the first thought of the day—now that's being alive.

It's not who you are, but what you're made of.
It's not where you come from, but where you're going to.

So much yet to be learned.

—Papa

6:30 a.m.
Bright and beautiful

The Art of Work and Working

Good Morning again, Little Ones,

I DECIDED TO START THIS DAY with another crack at the ever beckoning woodpile, going through these old dried pine cartwheels like a red devil on blue ice. You can really hear the cracking of the ax echoing off the far granite walls up valley. I know I'll need at least three or four cords to get through whatever I'm supposed to get through this fall or winter. Don't know how long I'll need to stay warm, but I'll be damned if I'm going to freeze to death on the way to my own dying.

Of course, working makes me think about working, which makes me want to write you about the art of work and working. Your old man has pulled his fair share of labor in his day. Earned my first wage-paying blisters at the tender age of thirteen pounding post for Brunt Richards up on his summer pasture—drove me harder than a rented mule putting up that fence line, but it sure made me tough. Was a bit of work gypsy in my young man years, digging fire lines with the Forest Service up in Montana, fencing for Possession

Ranch in the great state of Washington, and baling hay in eastern Idaho. Bartended, drove trucks, moved cattle, wrangled dudes, and built barns. Guided folks up to the top of mountains so they could say they'd been there and then hauled them back down to earth. Played my guitar when I needed a lunch or dinner and a few extra bucks. Also sold vegetable seeds and encyclopedias when the going got tough. Even edited a newspaper to work my brain for a spell. Nothing wrong with being young, working hard, and exploring life all at the same time.

Other folks might not call working an art, but when did I give an owl's two hoots about what other folks think. Let's put it this way: there are good ways, better ways, and bad ways to work. And like with anything else, I've got a few say-so's on what I think you two should know about work and working.

The number one rule of working is: DO THE BEST WORK YOU CAN. Why do something cobble-cocked that looks like it was built by drunken elves? Why do anything other than your best? What's the point? Think you can get away with doing less work by doing it half-assed? Maybe. But more often than not it will come back to bite you in the hindmost part when you have to do it all over again because you didn't do it right in the first place. Make doing your best a habit, and you'll never know not doing your best. If you build roads, then build them Roman—make them last two thousand years. Dig ditches as if you were taking them to the state fair to win another blue ribbon for best ditches. It's never a question of what you do but how well you do it.

A corollary to the number one work rule came, of course, from grandpa's well-oiled adage machine and was proclaimed whenever he left me to do a job by myself: "Work like you're shining God's shoes," (which left me with the kid conundrum of wondering if God really wore shoes, what they really would look like, and when was one supposed to stop shining?). I took grandpa's words to mean that you should do the best work you can, even if the boss never sees it—what matters is that you see it. Because ultimately you're your own boss.

The other number one rule of working is (yes, in your pa's world there can be two number one rules): FIND THE WORK YOU LOVE TO DO. Because, in my book, the greatest devil of them all is to work just for money. I know more miserable souls who, chasing the almighty buck through some strange loophole of logic, believe that the more money you have the happier you'll be. Generally I find that the richer they are, the wretcheder they become. Remember, work is like sleep. Since it takes up a third of your day, a third of your life, it's better to choose a job that you halfway enjoy than to be contentedly miserable as you curse your fate and count down the years (and your hoard) until you offhandedly meet the grand coffin-catcher himself, whereupon you greet the last moments of your life clutching a big bouquet of stupidity.

So ideally and someday you're going to discover (or it might discover you) what could be the job of your dreams. Yet soon you'll realize it's going to take years of hard work to fulfill that dream. Welcome to the world of sacrifice. What? No silver platter handed to you with your job on it? Your lucky horseshoe and Indian head penny aren't working? What? You're talented? So what! So is the rest of the world. As Mr. Flaubert put it so blithely, "Talent is nothing but long patience." NO ONE said it was going to be easy. If it were easy, then everybody else would be doing it. NO ONE can make you sacrifice. NO ONE can give you determination. You either do or don't—nothing else. To do is to succeed. To don't is not. It's your choice.

I never thought I could write for a newspaper, let alone edit one. But, as my high school teacher and mentor Mr. Conrad once told me, "If you're a writer, then write. Otherwise, go get a real job." I spent years, off and on, writing oddments, obits, and stockyard reports for spec before I got a chance to report for, and then become editor of, The Sentinel—one of my dream jobs (yes, you can have more than one).

The bossman is to work as spurs to the horse. The boss is a part of life like breathing, taxes, and death. And unless you happen to be the head honcho, more than likely you'll have your very own boss to boss you. Remember, you and the boss both have special jobs to do. Yours is to be on time and do your work well; otherwise you'll be out on your keister. Your boss's job is to make sure you do your job and do it right. If, however, your boss turns out to be some sort of lord of the manor, demeaning you in front of your fellow workers, overworking you like a slave, generally treating you like dirt, or otherwise proving himself a certifiable failure as a human being, then you have no choice left but to find a new boss or just get out of town. Remember, life is too short to be spent dancing with idiots.

Little Ones,

Had to take a mid-morning penman's break. Splitting wood and stacking words will get anybody to being hungry, including your old man. So I hightailed back to the cabin for some sourdough biscuits and what was left of this morning's "eye cleaner" (which, translated from grandpa's never-ending descriptionary, means "coffee"). Now your pa's refueled and anxious to put up a good day's supply of words. Back to the job of working...

Working outside is a great way to make a living. My feeling is that getting paid for doing what you like in the great outdoors is like receiving an extra hundred bucks in every paycheck. And if one gets paid for cowboying... they might as well pay angels to have wings. On this aspect of working I am contentedly biased.

Sometimes you're stuck with a part of your job you don't like. Well, even the job of your dreams might have a bit of dirt sticking to the oil pan. You can moan like a sick dog, or you can meet the challenge. Once again, you either do or you don't. But realize that gutting it out will get you nothing but admiration from your cohorts who are honest, hard-working folks themselves, all of whom realize what it's like to pull the dog detail sometime in their lives.

There's nothing wrong with not knowing how to do something at work. What's wrong is not asking questions about how to do it. If you think you'll look stupid for asking, just imagine how you'll look later when you're supposed to know what to do and can't do it. If someone gives you a hard time for asking, tell him you're trying to learn to do your job better. That will usually shut him up. But always ask. Ask. Ask.

Do not do anything that is unsafe. You will. I have. But if you get hurt on the job, you lose. If you're doing physical labor and have to pick up something heavy, use your legs and not your back. Like I mentioned yesterday, screw up your back and you'll learn about growing old fast. Think before you do anything that's risky. Unless you're getting paid to drive cars off a cliff or to ride bull elephants in heat, you <u>do</u> <u>not</u> have to injure yourself for the sake of a job. Keeping your health is everything—so that you can work longer (hmmmm), read more books, eat more steak, ride more horses, and befriend more champagne.

The BIG secret to work is to become good at working. Work hard. Go beyond what your supposed to do. When you're done with one job, ask for another. Gain a reputation for being a great worker because the bigger secret is that everyone will want to hire you, and you'll never be at a loss for work.

But working hard is not all there is to being good at working (and this is really the last big secret)—you have to work smart too. I remember back in my posthole-and-fencing days when I was a young man with a hard-earned moustache and as touchy as a teased snake, I suggested to this old coot that we weld some weight to the bottom of the pounder so as to help break through the hardpan dirt a little easier. "Afraid of working yourself too hard, boy?" he asked me. And my Welsh blood (and I'm sure an inkling of my Irish) replied, "Afraid of working too smart, old man?" (Your pa wasn't always exactly politic with his tongue, ignoring grandpa's advice that "your head is not just a place for your mouth to vacation.") And I guess my mouth and I weren't altogether too smart because my job and I had to part company soon thereafter.

Little Ones, the only way to truly learn how to work is to get out and do it. And your pa's advice on working is only as good as the misery you care to avoid. (Of course, what good is advice if we can't ignore it.) I hope that you two will find the best of work and working in your lives. Remember, work is what we all have to do. How we do it is the art of it all.

Papa

8:42 p.m.
Moon rising over the valley

Things I Don't Know

Evening, Little Ones,

THERE ARE MORE THINGS I don't even know by half than I do know by whole.

Thirty-three years has given me just so much perspective. And I will never know about the getting old.

There is so much yet to be learned. I'm not bitter about the past, the bad or the hurtful I've run into. I've been burned in business. My heart's been broken more than once. Many a close friend has gone over the ridge. Who hasn't been down this road before? I've felt the knife's edge, been shot at, and have seen evil and good in more places than I ever could imagine. But I'm still hopeful. To live longer. To continue to love deeply. To learn more and more—and more beyond that. Even to hold you two someday. We'll see.

I'm saying you can't know it all, and you shouldn't. You'd probably explode from knowing too much.

Respect both what you need to know and what you don't need to know. Respect mystery, for mystery is still needed to run the universe.

Older doesn't always mean wiser. It just means that you've had more time to do the same things over and over again—right, wrong, and different.

The things you don't know or understand are as important as your desire to know them. This is the relationship of man to mystery.

If you don't know, ask.

If you don't know, listen.

If you don't know, watch.

There's so much to learn. So much to enjoy. So terribly much to be curious about. Take your life and run with it. Make a habit of being alive. This much of anything, I have learned. And am still learning.

—Papa

Night—rain stopped.
Slight northwesterly breeze

Little Ones,

ONCE UPON A TIME your papa wrote and played music for people. For him it was a dance on the moon and the cat's pajamas. He couldn't imagine being any happier than when words and notes arrived together. Such a strangely beautiful sensation when a song poured out of him. As if each was a first and last song. Yet when another song arrived, he knew that heaven had smiled again.

He felt he had been given a gift but didn't know why. But the why wasn't as important as the doing. So he gave his songs to family and friends and that's how he honored his gift. He especially enjoyed singing for your mom. She heard the rough and the finished of many a song. And I could always count on her smile, and sometimes even a kiss at the end. What your pa wouldn't do for that smile—and that kiss. I would play for her when she was outside watering the plants or even when she was taking a bath. I would even serenade her to sleep at night. And still she would smile, even in her sleep.

My guitar has stood by me for more years than I can remember. Saved me when I needed saving—even when I didn't know I needed saving. Pretty much a second heart. When all is said and done, this guitar will be yours to keep. She's given me many songs. I traded an old '56 Ford pickup with a locked-up engine and a rusted-out muffler for her. That was the best darn deal I ever made—besides meeting your mom. I scratched all those names and dates and quotes and pictures on it because… well, it just seemed to me that's what this guitar wanted.

I know your mother will bring you to music as I would have. Maybe one of you will play this guitar someday. Maybe.

I have written several new songs in the last few weeks. Wrote one last night. They're different than any I've ever written. Perhaps because this is a different time. My guess is that they are letters wanting to be music. I will give them to you when I'm finished.

At some point, please pass these songs on to my compadre Painter Al. I'm sure he'd love to hear them. (He's a tough character to track down but your mom will know where to find him.) We were two peas in a pod making the music come alive. He might even enjoy taking these songs on the road. He's a great musician, one hell of a guitar player—and as good a friend as they come. And he loves music the same way I do.

Papa

Birthing and Raising Kids

Dear Little Ones,

I DON'T KNOW MUCH about kids except that I was one once. The only in-depth experience I've had with babies is changing the diapers of your Uncle Tom and your Uncle Adam when they were only half as big as nothing, that and constantly pushing on the top of your Uncles Mike's head, following the logic befitting any child that if I pushed steadily enough and long enough he would grow up to be a dwarf, which would help prolong the pecking order that I, as first-born and king of the roost, was spending the better part of my childhood perpetuating. Being twins, you probably won't have to worry about sibling coup d'états, or being asked to slice up the dinner's last chunk of pot roast into four perfectly equal portions, surgery necessary to fairly serve the constantly hungry wolves that we were. Actually most of my kid-time was spent in doing chores, playing in the woods, getting into and out of trouble (which is the natural state of grace for all boys), and being on the graze for more feed.

But I can tell you this much—my ma and pa, your grandma and grandpa, are the two best parents that fate and Providence could ever have bestowed upon me. Just follow their example when you get lost in any of your trailblazings. Your mom is also a natural with kids, and I've watched her in fascination as she tamed the wildest rug boars imaginable. So, between the three of them, and whatever tidy scraps of advice I throw in, you should get a good handle on how to have and raise kids.

The first and foremost rule: Don't have kids until you're ready. And when you do have them, have them all the way. They aren't like some Cadillac that you can turn back into the dealership after three years. You're in for a long and beautiful haul. If you have any doubts, don't have the little toadstools. It's a fool who thinks that having a kid is a right, which is the biggest crock of fish-heads I've ever heard. You have a responsibility, not only to a person but also to a spirit because that's what a child is. A pissing, crying, yawning, giggling, laughing pack-age of spirit that is looking for you to take the lead. It's a heck of a responsibility to look after a spirit. So give kids the best of who you are. That's the most you can ever do. And remember, you don't own them like horses, dogs, or pet roosters. You don't get to keep them for-ever. They move on. And it's your job to let them move on. And if you've done your job in the right way, they'll come back. They'll learn that their blood is all they can truly rely on in this world.

Ma and pa had three hard-and-fast rules. Don't lie, don't steal, and don't come in later than six o'clock for supper. It doesn't matter exactly what the three rules are, just as long as you have three rules that you stand by. I've seen more brats per square inch from folks not taking charge and letting kids know where the boundaries are. Part of loving kids is laying down fencelines. They need to know immediately when they've crossed a line; otherwise the lesson doesn't get learned. You're doing kids wrong when you don't let them know that they've done wrong. Life is about actions and consequences. I may sound old-fashioned, but there's something to be said for a thousand and more years of fence building.

Love your kids and just be there for them. You don't have to eyeball their every moment or to orchestrate all their comings and goings. They know this. They know that's too much. All they want is to be assured that there's a home fire cooking, that there are two foremen and a rulebook, and that there's someone to tuck them in at night.

Don't spoil kids by trying to buy them off, to buy their time. Kids aren't stupid. They know a bribe when they see one. They want a parent, not a payoff. They don't care if you're jack-king-rodeo or mister-you-own-New-York. All they understand is time spent with you or without you. It's that simple.

Read to kids. Read to them. Read to them.

Teach them what you love to do in life. It really doesn't matter what it is. Just show them how important a passion is.

Ride with them. Teach them how to saddle up young.

Camp with them. Take them out into fields and forests. Especially if you choose to live in a city. Kids are meant to get dirty and run loose and find bugs and build forts and splash in streams and lakes and... you get the picture.

Teach them most definitely how to say thank you and please. (I think we've already covered that.)

Teach them about fairness. What justice is. What sharing means.

Answer their questions when they have questions.

Don't put them off and kill any part of their curious spirit. Don't ever do that. To me, that's as great a sin as any.

Make no mean no. Not maybe no. Not half no. Just no.

Kids are kids and not little adults. They're watching and listening to you all the time. They're figuring out the game plan but still don't know all the rules. Talk straight to them and they'll respect you for it.

Teach them not to talk back. Learning respect for one's elders seems to be a dying art form. It's a well-trained imp that has learned he can talk back.

Teach them to clean their rooms and look after their own animals.

Give them chores and teach them how to earn their keep. The sooner they learn this, the better off they'll be when they leave the nest.

Teach them love and respect by the love and respect you show to your husband or wife.

Laugh a lot with them. They're laughing machines. Wind them up and watch them go.

Love them the best way you can and that love will come back tenfold.

When they get to be of driving age, make sure that their first car is a big old highway car. It's a great coat of armor for a rookie driver.

If they want to learn about drinking, smoking, or chewing, join them in a bottle of Jack Daniels, a carton of Marlboros, or a half dozen cans of Copenhagen, and let them heave their guts out. Nothing like taking the fun out of their vices.

Don't teach your kids to fear being honest with you. They should be able to talk to you about anything or ask for your help at any time. If you nail them hard enough for speaking the truth, they'll learn not to go down that road again. It's like making a horse head-shy by cuffing him once too often.

Encourage them to learn another language—Spanish, French, Norwegian, Russian or Bantu. Start them when they're too young to know any better.

Teach them about sex before they learn about sex what they shouldn't know about sex.

Take them traveling whenever you get the chance—wherever, however… Throw yourselves around the world. There are Eskimos and minarets and narwhales and mangoes and…

Give them music. Any and all sorts. Teach them an instrument. If you want them to play an instrument, make sure you don't force them. Worst idea in the world. Music should be a labor of love, not an act of slavery. Above all, never kill the music spirit in them if they have it. That's another cardinal sin in my eyes.

Teach them about the Golden Rule. Teach them how to pray. Give them God in the mountains and the forests and throw in a handful of prayers for them to learn. Bring them to the Good Book, to gather what they will from it. Teach them to be tolerant of other people's ways of believing in God. There's nothing worse than high-hat folks who think they've got God's ear only to themselves.

Good, bad, or otherwise, this is my two bits worth

on bringing up kids. This is more or less how I'd raise you two. I know there's more to say, but I just can't think of it right now. Besides, my brain's all worn out, my belly's growling for an early supper, and the evening is begging for a walk in the meadow.

Love,
Papa

Full Moon

THESE MOMENTS CASCADE upon one another. There is so little time. I write until there is no more to write. And then I go out into the long meadows and walk until I can walk no more. Out here I listen. Under skies and mountains large and comforting, Here at shepherd's dusk, in a valley without echo, I listen for you. With a frayed longing, I hear your shadow voice whispering within me from far away. I grasp at what is left of this husky sun lying golden upon the upper meadows of lodgepole and bear grass. I gather the last remnants of the evening's breeze, so cool and lazy within my arms, feeling it curl up like a small and innocent kitten. And I see that behind a cloak of clouds, dalliance suits the canting moon.

Suddenly I do not wish to lose another moment, and I covet all pristine light.

July 24
8:30 a.m.
Rain

Rain's Great

Morning, Little Ones,

I'M ON MY SECOND CUP of coffee with the door wide open, huddled next to the potbelly stove. How much better does being alive get then sitting beside a warm fire amidst a misty rainy morning. I wish and I wish and I wish you were here to see this all.

I love rain. I love to walk in it, run through it. If I could—and I have—I would run around in the rain as naked as a peacock, except when it snow-rains, which makes it a wee bit too cold to bare one's outers.

I like the rain when it's really pouring cats and monkeys, and you can see everyone in their cars scowling crankily like years-old tar paper curling and cracking around the edges of its misuse.

Rain with no shoes is just as much fun as rain with big rubber galoshes.

When it rains too hard, schools should have rain

days like they have snow days, and cancel school altogether. Then you could go and splash to your heart's content, instead of being sequestered in some gummy, humid sweatbox of a classroom while it spills and pours outside. Of course, this idea isn't practical for states like Washington and Oregon, where you would learn too little and play too much. It probably wouldn't pass muster with many parents either. But what the heck, it's a grand notion to consider.

Rain with an umbrella is just as appealing as rain without an umbrella. Rain with an umbrella while holding hands with your lover is damned sure nice.

And I don't care what age you are, kissing in the rain is the best.

Rain on the top of your head is a mighty fine sensation. Especially when it's summer, and the sun is hot over there and all the rain is pouring down over here.

A hot shower or a long, sultry hot bath is mucho fantastico after you've been drenched like a dog—preferably by your own shenanigans rather than by a Mack truck.

Rain is delicious when you're inside the house next to the fireplace, and its fire is crackling away in a fine madness, hissing and spitting. Rain on the roof of your tent is pioneer and romantic. Rain on the roof of your bedroom at two a.m. is as comforting as an old friend who comes over for a visit and a hot cup of coffee, and you both kick around a conversation or two for a few or many hours. Yes, and a steady rain and rooftop, and a warm bed and a loved one, all make for paradise.

Heavy rains and a good book. A perfect extravagance.

Country music, a working heater, and a new pair of windshield wipers makes a rain drive as tasty as a peach-pie spring on a church-day porch.

Thunder and lightning with a tumble of rain is even better than just rain in my Bible. And if you toss in a hefty bellow of wind and uproar, then you have the finest culmination of nature's perambulations that can and will ever grace your pretty wet heads and glossy eyes.

Rain. Tumble, bumble, and fall on me. Any old day, any old way. Come for a visit, or come for a stay. Rain, rain, don't go away.

And as much as I love rain, I also love the day after a rain when the sky has been scoured clean and all the stars have been polished to a keen glimmer. The ranch smells like spring-autumn when the broad earth releases every spice it has to offer. People smile. Quinky little ions in the air all sputter around your head, making you feel giddy for no obvious reason. That's rain for you.

If you go too long without rain, you'll get rain fever and then it's imperative that you find the nearest possible storm cloud, place yourself under it, and get a large dose of rain for an extended period of time. In this way you will temporarily avoid madness or sadness, or any form of paranoia, common to those who have gone without rain for way too long.

I hope you two come to like rain as much as your pa did. I love rain, and I'm really going to miss it. Yes, I will miss it.

—Papa

Night and rain...

Little Ones,

IT'S BEGUN TO RAIN AGAIN, and there's a leak in the far corner of the cabin. A small coffee can is catching the drops. A mosquito that I can hear but can't see is moving in slow, yawing circles above my head but doesn't seem overly interested in making contact. I can hear my local sidekick, the mouse, scribbling and rummaging in another corner of the room, making more fit and non-sense. Most likely, in some midnight foray, he'll scamper across my face and scare the who-done-it out of me. Rain, mosquito, mouse. Rain, mosquito, mouse. Sounds like the opening refrain of a bad Busby Berkley musical.

The tea sitting on my desk is still hot, black tea with a shimmy of sugar. If I had the cream, I'd add a dollop of it, but no such luck. I can't grow cream, and I don't think the local bob-tail deer would enjoy a good teat squeezing. That is, if I could rope one of them, which I couldn't. That mosquito I heard has finally landed somewhere else, rather than on me. The rain continues to pour outside. It looks like we're in for a real gully washer today. Or as cowboy Charlie used to put it, "a real frog strangler."

I wonder what you look like, Little Ones. Whose hair did you get? And your eyes? Ice-blue or earth-brown? Whose jaw and ears did you take? Do you inherit your mother's Mediterranean mouth and gypsy sway, or did fate ply you with my Welshman's nose and bull-bridged canter? Whose stubbornness did you catch? Or did you get a double dose? Were you given your mother's serene smile that could melt my wild soul at any given moment? Did you happen upon my pipe fitter palms and my piano fingers? I always wondered myself where I got those from.

Whom will you marry? Will they be a lover, companion, and friend? Will you propose, or be proposed to, in a magical place? Under the northern lights or atop the Eiffel Tower? Will you cry, and will you laugh—and most certainly you and your lover will look deeply into each other's eyes and know why you must stay together forever.

How will you live? On a ranch, or in the city, or both? Will you raise cowboys, or doctors, or both? Will you have mountains to watch over you, or skyscrapers, or both? Will you walk in the quiet and cool of an autumn day through the meadows on your ranch, or will you stroll down some promenade, gazing at shop windows filled with things wondrous and singular?

What will you know? What will you seek? Will you know the hunger for knowledge and the desire for a vision? Will these be in your blood? Will you seek the prowess of destiny with all the bittersweet loneliness that attends those who choose to lead? Will you explore the myriad incarnations of beauty and truth as they exist within you and beyond? Will you grasp the quietness in your life, and recognize the treasure and divinity of the small when it is given to you?

Who will be your friends, for life and for the moment? Will you recognize the sharks that lie in wait for your trust and loyalty? Will you ever know the stabbing of betrayal, or the shattering of your heart? What will be your fears, and who will be your ghosts? What darkness will you know, and what god will you come to?

Who will you be, my Little Ones? Will you dance for the fires of your youth and run at midnight to water's edge, diving into summer's heat? Will you ride a wild mare to any thought or dream or love of your making? Will you seek the artistry of your own infatuations and explore all the reckless and eccentric corners of your own impetuous world?

Will you do, and not wait? Will you listen when it is time to listen? Will you give the deepest of your courage and the most understanding of your love to others? Will you hold the hand that needs to be held, and be patient with the hurt that must continue to hurt? Will you know to grieve deeply when that moment is upon you, and to find those that will guard you and care for you when you are wounded?

I wonder what you will be. It is like a Christmas present that I can never open. Always to wonder what is inside. What is the hope? What is the possibility? What alluring brightness glimmers within the beribboned package? What tickling irony? It puts the biggest damn grin on my face. I will be content to know that your mother will be the one to unveil the gift for both of us.

I wonder.
I wonder.
I wonder.

—Papa

August 1

4:20 a.m.
36 degrees

Time—The First and Last Gift

Little Ones,

TIME, WE ARE ONLY given so much of it. In the big picture—the gargantuan, universal, cosmological infinity-infinity picture—there's quite a bit of time. But in the small geological puff of a lifetime, we don't even rate an eye-blink.

Time. It's our most precious resource. We forget how rare time is until we realize how little we have left. Like your last gasp for air under water—only then do you realize how much you love to breathe. It's a dog-trick of our nature not to appreciate what we have in front of us until it is taken away from us or lost. Then we grasp and clutch pathetically at our last scraps of time, or breath, or love without so much as a hint that we've learned a damn thing about anything.

Time—the most valuable gift, next to life, that you will ever be given. More precious than gold. And you should squander gold before you throw away time.

Because time is the greatest currency we are given to spend, and how we spend it becomes The Big Question. Yet because we have not earned time, we do not give it much value. We humans are squirrely like that.

Time. We all want as much of it as we can get. Yet, the wanting of the much is not as important as being alive to what we already have. In the vernacular of big business, it's a quality-versus-quantity issue.

"I'm so busy I just don't have time."

Don't have time for what?

To take your kids to the circus?

To have a picnic with your wife—without the kids?

To smoke a good cigar with a close friend?

To re-read your favorite novel?

To take a mountain hike by yourself?

You can busy yourself right into a sweet dark grave and, only at the last moment of small change and diminished air, regret not having spent more time living. Busying yourself by filling your calendar with the sparrows-feet scritchings of a busy-bee lifetime. By endlessly carting your kids to their next umpteenth event like a momified taxi service—creating mere kid-cogs in the family manufacturing machine. By having to work at two jobs—the two-and-a-half hour, fifty-week-a-year commute and the one you make your living at but don't like. By keeping up with the Joneses and the Smiths and the Vandersnorts, spending more time spending, and not enough time figuring out how to live without spending.

So have a near brush with death:

Like getting ptomaine poisoning while having pneumonia.

Like almost being mistaken for a seven-point buck during hunting season.

Like almost crashing your car on the way to a funeral.

Like discovering the adrenaline mathematics of a massive bull bearing down on you like some angry meteorite while you hightail it toward the nearest fenceline.

Like feeling your heart fly out of your throat as you fall through the snow in a whiteout—only to discover you're roped over the edge of a hundred-foot crevasse.

If any of the aforementioned happens to you, then you will truly comprehend what time is worth, and how greedy you are for more of it.

Near death is not a sure-fire way to wake you up, but at least it will spark a flame in the darkness of your brain, in a life that we mostly bumble through.

Time. Either you're for it or against it. So be here now. Not later. Do what you want to do, and with the people you love. Learn to appreciate time and make doing so a habit. And if you want to do nothing, then enjoy doing it well. Why do anything by half? Why live a life diluted? What's the use?

What good is a Gibson with only two onions?

What good is an "I love You," if said only when you have to?

What good is it to ride a horse if you cannot gallop? What good is it to believe in someone if you doubt your own belief?

Time. Either you're with it or you're not. So stop right now. Sit your Brunswick down and take a good look at the rest of the minutes in your hour and day. Regard them all as heaven-sent. For that's what they are. This first and last gift.

Your time is your time. Be awake to it. It's hard work to be wisely alive.

Papa

Dusk
On top of Echo's Ridge

Little Ones,

I GAZE AT THESE giant blue mountains surrounding me, now reddening in the dusk of evening. I look out across the spaciousness before me and feel a small measure of contentment, for I know my demons and devils have an adequate playground in which to bump their big heads together and battle it out.

My thoughts. So much clearer here and now. It is important to feel tiny and useless against such magnificence. Humbled, I am learning to face the immensity of it all. As a doe in the underbrush, I find refuge within the vastness of these rocks and valleys. I feel safe to wonder. Where the unknown begins, and I with it.

—Papa

About ten minutes after sunrise
38 degrees

My Two Bits on Growing Old

Dear Little Ones,

GOOD MORNING—AGAIN! The corrals today are a circus. Decided to move my pen outdoors for sunup, only to encounter a couple of young crows playing king-of-the-fencepost, frolicking around like a couple of air otters. Since they're somewhat new at feathered flight, they can't always make the top of the post without half falling over.

Seems like a thousand years ago and yesterday that I was out here at first light with grandpa, saddling our horses to ride the day's fence line or look over the herd. Once or twice a summer we'd get to go to town, always heading out in the morning dark because the ride was a good twenty miles away.

I remember one strange day. A movie day—where everything was slightly more perfect than perfect. The sky, my horse, the temperature. Even the trees and birds and water got in on the act. It was just like the movies, but I was in it. And in keeping with the movie-ness of the day, Grandpa suddenly, in a fit of Spartacus-to-the-throng theatrics, proclaimed to the sagebrush, pine, meadows, and me, "Old is for old people."

Little Ones, you have to understand that Grandpa being Grandpa, and his also being a cowboy, pretty much excluded him from dramatic voice-raising, arm-flailing, or face gesticulating. So, surprised by this outburst and not fully appreciating the machinations of the adult mind, I asked him what he meant. "Just what I said, boy. Old is for old people," and with that, he spurred his horse Cayenne and tore across the meadow in a mad gallop, leaving me no matter of speculation as to what devilish gravitational whirligations had been bottled up inside him.

After twenty years, I've finally got an inkling of what made gramps gallop off as if a swarm of wild Indians was after his scalp. I know I don't near qualify as an expert on getting old, but I've sure got my own Indians motivating me to move fast.

Little Ones, in honor of grandpa and his outburst, here's your pa's two bits on the yeas and nays of growing old:

The trick to <u>not</u> growing old is to:
Stay curious.
Keep your teeth.
Stay hopeful.
Do everything gracefully, yet kick when you have to.

If you believe the numbers, then you're old.
If you don't believe the numbers and believe in your spirit, then you're ageless.

Growing old isn't about age. I've seen people in their twenties who were old.

All you have to do to quickly become old is to slowly give up being alive.

Old is believing, "I'm too old for that."

Ignore your health and you'll get old. At any age. Somewhere in the near past, I remember telling you about being, "as young as your spine is supple." This idea makes sense. So keep the body moving and get some air into the lungs. The body is like any machine. You have to oil it and keep its parts moving.

If you don't know how to grow old, don't start learning how to grow old.

Being old is for grumps, crabby-heads, and whiners whose main goal is to drag everyone and everything down into their miserable knothole. Ignore the bastards.

All you have to do is to look into someone's eyes to know if they're old or not. Don't go by their age. Check to see if someone's alive in there. You'll know… Just because you're breathing, doesn't mean you're alive.

Old is old at any age. Old is when you quit asking questions about this, that, and everything. Old is when you forget how to love—or worse, don't care. Old is when you don't want to dance anymore. Old is when you don't want to learn anything new except how to be old. Old is when people tell you that you are old—and you believe them.

Dying—everybody has to do. But being old, well hell that's your choice.

Pa

When You're Eighteen, Do Not Read This

Little Ones,

D O NOT READ THIS. Because now that you're eighteen, you are supposed to (according to Greek myth, Freud, and your pa) do exactly the opposite of what your parents want you to do (although I've probably hooked you into reading this far). Besides, when you're eighteen, you won't need to read this. You are now divine in your wisdom, immortal in your body, and perfectly decisive in all matters relating to your general existence. Now knowing as much as you do about how the universe works, you have no real reason to read your old man's words—especially because they are from your old man and they are old. So do as I say—help your old man, and please don't read this letter...

EIGHTEEN? Why not nineteen or twenty-one? Or sixteen for that matter? Because the powers-that-be figured that by eighteen you've become so full of the preciousness of your own existence that it's best for you to get out of Dodge before the light of your magnificent young essence overwhelms everyone in your path. In short, IT'S TIME to GROW UP. Who wants to be continually ordered around like some junior lackey scrubbing the decks or scraping off barnacles? Who wants to be regulated like some underage prisoner of war, being told when you can eat, sleep, or breathe for that matter. No, IT'S TIME for you to be the captain of your own ship, sailing wherever your desires and the winds of fortune take you. IT'S TIME for you to escape from prison and taste the bountiful fruits of freedom.

As a kid, I once heard a fully-feathered and upright adult bleat, "When I grow up—" "And that's all my little ears could handle. In my entire career as a child, Little Ones, I'd never heard such downright ludicrous, mushmouth cacklegaffel. WHY wouldn't you want to grow up? WHY wouldn't you want to be an adult? NO MORE naps in the prime of day. NO MORE eating boiled Brussels sprouts, or fried liver, or pickled pigs feet. NO MORE doing Saturday morning barn chores, or hauling in the after-school Monday-Wednesday-Friday-and-Sunday firewood, or taking out the daily garbage, or feeding the horses, chickens, and dogs every night, of every week, of every year.

WHY wouldn't you want to do whatever, whenever, however, and with whomever. Stay up seven nights a week if that's your whim and tickle. Eat French Fries, banana splits, and chocolate-covered anythings until you're the size of a bull moose. Go anywhere at any-time—to a Trojan's football game or to Pete's bowling alley; to the Wagon Wheel or Betty Mapleson's house; to Kansas or New York by rail or by horse; by tramp steamer to Ceylon or by aeroplane to Peking.

Okay, so all I saw were the bright lights of adult-hood, but being an adult, and getting there as fast as I could seemed a far better deal than staying a kid forever. Or as Aunt Lynnette once, in a fit of loving exasperation, put it to me, "You were just born wanting to grow up." And for once, as a kid, I knew exactly what that meant.

EIGHTEEN—and now you are free. *FREE, FREE, FREE!* Free to stomp on the clock, stay out all night, and drink like you're at hell's only watering hole. Free to be half-witted, silly-foolish, and imbecilic in any order you want. Free to freckle around the fields as naked as Adam's first tuxedo and bugle like a bull elk in rutting season. Oh, the lush glory of such unfettered freedom. What nobody tells you and what's hidden in the fine, fine print of adulthood is that you are now free to go to war, free to sign contracts and be sued over them, and free to be locked up in jail (as an adult). You are now in the eyes of the society and all its laws a legal adult. You are free to be responsible and irresponsible with no one to blame but yourself. How's them bananas?

You are now masters of your own fate and are free

to screw it up any which way you want. You can also *not* screw it up any which way you want. Either way, it's your choice. So it's time to buck up and become a real, bona fide adult. Sounds scary? Well, it is if your folks raised you to be a thumb-sucker, holding on to momma's apron strings and papa's hand-me-outs. But if your folks raised you as an adult-in-training, to one day take charge of your life, then with a smidtchel of trepidation, a smarter of fear, and more enthusiasm than a summer sea of spring seals, becoming eighteen will be a long-awaited, triumphal glory day. Good God almighty, how great can that be.

Now you're EIGHTEEN and IT'S TIME! IT'S TIME for you get off the dime, scoot, scram, skedaddle, clear out bag and baggage, pull up stakes, up-anchor, haul tail, take wing, scratch gravel, scallyhoot, pull foot, shove in the clutch, break camp, get on the horse, mosey, sashay, shake the pegs, and blow town. IT'S TIME for you grow up, get out, and go. It's time to put away the beads and the baubles of childhood for the freedoms and responsibilities of becoming and being an adult. And nothing could be more unnerving, daunting, terrifying, and magnificently wonderful in the whole wide world for you at this very moment.

And what, Little Ones, is your foremost obligation, job, duty, and commitment as sparkling new adults? To be responsible for your own freedom! What? Responsible and freedom go together? At eighteen? Damn right.

You're now free to make your own destiny—choosing how free you want to be. Because everything you do now is your OWN choice. And you can also not choose—and that is your choice. And that's the magic, fear, and beauty of being a real adult. To fall or fly by your own choice. The responsibility to become—or not become.

Sometimes, Little Ones, so much free freedom is more free than most people know what to do with. Some folks take only baby steps, like small birdlets practicing their take-offs and landings right close to the nest. Others get a taste of the wild wind right from the first flap, gorging themselves on their new-found ability to go wherever, whenever, and however they please. And others sadly never really leave the cradle and confines of childhood, fearing their day of emancipation and shackled to the family cage with a debilitating combination of ignorance, indulgence, and love, all because their parents want perpetual playmates, rather than raising grownups-to-be. Is it scary to leave the nest? You bet. But worse yet is hanging on to the last twigs of childhood, never trusting the god-given fact that you were actually and always meant to fly.

And sometimes you'll never realize how much freedom you truly have been given until you've given it all away (and you'll only know that when you're usually much older and have fettered away your freedoms as if the party balloons were endless and somehow, if let go, would always fly back to the party).

Eighteen—Now what do you do? Learn the machinery of being an adult. The intricacies of weaving together your freedoms and your responsibilities to create a brand new you. Think of turning eighteen as the day you were born to be an adult. And from this day forward you're going to learn how to be the best adult you can be. When you were a child, you learned to be a child, but now you must learn to be more than your age. Because even though you are eighteen, it doesn't mean you're actually grownup. Yes, legally you're an adult. But legal doesn't confer instant smarthood or ooo-ahh maturity. You have to earn the right to be an adult by practicing, learning, and trying to be the best adult you can be.

Remember, it's still a mystery to be an adult. If you knew it all before eighteen, you'd have nothing to look forward to. Besides, to be wise and eighteen is as possible as catching lightning in a bottle...

You're eighteen—

Now get out of town and see the world. The bigger the picture you can see, the more you'll realize how big the picture really is. Travel, travel, travel.

No one owes you a thing. So don't expect it. You're on your own.

Don't get married—yet. Dream. Dream big. At

least once, pull out the stops on something in your life. Maybe twice. Get an education—by book or by school, and by life. Play. Have great friends to live, work, and play with. And to make great memories. And to share life with. And have fun. And even more fun. You have the rest of your life to not have fun. Love once or twice—deeply once and with great regret, or not. Settle down only when you're ready to settle down. No sooner. Then when you do find yourself a loving husband or wife, be the greatest of friends.

Making both good and stupid mistakes is your job. Hopefully the good mistakes will teach you and the stupid mistakes won't hurt you (too much).

Sometimes the best way is to get out of your own way.

Be the same person—with or without money.

Enjoy the ride now. You'll be successful later, however you define success.

Don't complain—you haven't earned the right.

As an adult, be child-like as you learn but not childish as you live.

And because you're eighteen, you still have more to gain in the world than you know to lose. Once you begin to understand regret and have memory of loss—of what can never be again—then you will be eighteen no longer.

Eighteen and your parents—
Your mama and papa weren't just born outright

mommas and papas. I know it's hard to believe but we actually had to grow up just like you, become eighteen just like you, and learn the hard way—just like you. You'll be amazed, upon turning eighteen, how little we parents seem to know about life and living, but as you quickly become older, you'll be more amazed at how quickly we seem to learn, as our ignorance turns miraculously to wisdom. So, Little Ones, if by suspending any or all of your eighteen-year-old time/space momentum for just one fraction of a moment and reading this letter (and listening to your mom), there exists the slight possibility you might avoid half the traps and discover but a few more fortunes of wisdom than your old man ever did, as you become a rightful citizen of your own Rome.

Say thank you. A child may forget to say thank-you but you are not a child now. And part of your responsibility as an adult is to learn how to say thank you, by both word and by action. The words are the respect for what you are given, and the actions—in becoming the best possible you—is the gratitude of a lifetime, the most profound thank-you any parent can and will ever know.

Will you ever truly understand us parents? Will you ever wonder or care how great or fallible we are? How wonderful or not? Yes, thank god, there is such a day, and for all parents this is Thanksgiving, Christmas, and the Fourth-of-July all rolled into one. Like some massive jungle flower blooming once every hundred years, your heretofore dormant understanding of us will only, and suddenly, awaken with the arrival of your own children, when hopefully your tired-eyed awe will skyrocket into fireworks of gratitude as you suddenly comprehend the massive amount of turmoil, grief, sleepless nights, gnashing teeth, heartache, heartache, and general worry, dread, and consternation that you once gave to us parents, which will now be your legacy. And of course, you will also be bequeathed all the great wonderment, love, and pride that comes with such a legacy, which means that the circle of being a true parent remains ever unbroken.

Eighteen—

The danger of this time… Beware of the insidious compromises of adulthood. The point at which you begin to compromise who and what you are. And what's really amazing is how easily we convince ourselves that we're not compromising but merely riding a horse that won't buck. It's your basic feel-good shortcut. Or lazy turn of the wheel. Or ever reassuring I'll-do-it-tomorrow. And soon enough you've become a connoisseur of your own concessions. And you're never fully aware that, like a single drop of water which leaves no impression, an eon of waterdrops creates a Grand Canyon. And that small rivulet of compromises once made, can someday become a lifetime flood of unhappiness.

You do have a choice (yes, back to choice) and the

key is to think. And I mean THINK, THINK, THINK, then DO. Even if you do just one think, you're ahead. A wisdom itch is what grandpa called it. It's when you're ready to pull a knucklehead and do something that you might regret, that you'll get this little itch of wisdom desperately trying to tell you to think. And if you stop for just one moment, (which is half an eternity to an eighteen-year old as I vaguely remember) and allow yourself a tiny appetizer of wisdom, you might not end up eating an entire plate of stupidity.

Eighteen—

My Little Ones. You have no idea how grand you are. Having all the world before you in incredible feast and endless pageantry. You are mischievous with curiosity, filled with stallion energy, and full of God's everything. You have no idea of death. No concept of ending. You are all beginning again—as you should be. You haven't completed the disappointment of not doing, nor the failing of not trying. You have not earned your tragedies—hopefully, not yet. You haven't discovered the sublime pain of heartache nor endured the life-pounding loss of a loved one. You don't know the unbounded ways in which life can be taken away from you or beaten out of you. You don't know, and thus ignorance is your wisdom and innocence is your strength, and both are your greatest blessing, and that's why you're eighteen. Now go and be the greatest of who you were meant to be. Life goes on ferociously—with or without you. It is your choice. Truly and magnificently your choice.

Papa

3:00 p.m.
68 degrees

Take A Walk

Afternoon, Little Ones,

WHERE AM I NOW? Here. Where I'm supposed to be. Going nowhere with good reason. Out in the great outside, in the farness and fetchness of it all. Far from all thoughts of marriage, love, and the like. Hiking through the puffy white clouds of a miniature heaven which is actually a field of tall blooming yampa. I know you both would like this. Your eyes barely above the flowers, strolling along like a couple of Munchkins on their way to a birthday party. Sure is nice to be out here in this glorious summer afternoon. It'll be autumn soon enough.

This walking—and going nowhere with necessity— reminds me of my ma and pa taking walks after supper. As a kid, I never quite understood (probably because I was a kid) why anyone would want to take walks anyhow. How boring. How adult. Why walk when you could run, ride, skip, trip, climb, scramble, crawl, or loiter with purpose. But then I'd never thought I'd like kissing girls, drinking whiskey, or eating mashed goose liver.

So what better place than here and now—with pen in hand, and with no destination and with great purpose, to talk my walk to you both.

Little Ones,

Take a walk.

To get out of the house and away from small walls and stuffy air.

To get away from the phone and radio and television, and all things electronic emitting sound or utilizing photon beams.

When you have the urge to see some sky.

To move your body and feel all your muscles.

To enjoy the wind, the rain, the sun, and all other assorted natural happenstances and byproducts.

To clear your head of cobwebs and lifewebs and thiswebs and thatwebs.

To suck some air down into your lungs and remind yourself that you have lungs to suck air down into.

To be quiet with yourself.

Take a walk to be quiet.

Take a walk.

To think about all the grand, the lofty, and the august happenings of the universe, and then take another walk to forget everything and just enjoy the walk.

Take a walk with a dog.

Take a walk with a good friend to talk out problems
of love and war, business and dreams.

Whenever you are sad or unhappy.

To see what nature is up to.

Take a walk.

At sunset with someone or no one.

At sunrise just as the stars are retiring.

In the rain, with your rain jacket and your rain boots
on to keep you dry.

With your lover, walking hand in hand, for a long,
long ways.

Take a walk.

To find out where the crows are hanging out.

To visit a friend's house, the corner store, the
library, or someplace where you don't have to go by car.

To celebrate most anything.

Take a walk with an old friend you haven't seen for
many moons and really catch up on life.

Take a walk to plan and plot, devise and design, the
reaching of your dreams.

To remember what is good in your life, and then
take another walk to make the thought stick.

Take a walk.

At any old time, for all these reasons or none, the sole and unremitting purpose being simply to take a walk.

So, take a walk.

Papa

Little Ones,

PERFECT. Such a calm moment I have not felt for a long time. Regal. Like a prince who has earned his day's keep and can reflect upon his land and people in a paradise given, green like an England of oaks and thrushes and rock walls made by ancient farmers and their dutiful sons. Why is this moment so perfect? Who decided to muzzle the black minutes of my black days for this priceless interlude? But let's not question the luck of yattering poets or warriors crossing Tiburons, for theirs is not to reason why—nor mine to even reason…

I spy a mermaid-green I have never seen before— embroidered in the white throne cloud above me. At its cotton edge a puckish sun refracts, hides, and reappears. Such a jeweled chance is being granted. A moment to rest below the high-wire of my remaining existence. To breathe sweet oxygen from both mortal glacier and nimble brook. To feel the cold-mountain and hot-day breeze upon my face. To smell the summer-baked pine and sage. Such elation I have not allowed myself for some time. Is this what happiness looks like? Like the long-forgotten smile upon a most enchanting face?

Somewhere in the corner stack of old grey-sleeved 78's that grandpa left here hides the Nutcracker Suite by Mr. Tchaikovsky. Your grandpa—who learned from both kings and commoners. I yearn for a stately moment that deserves the dignified horns of the Waltz of the Flowers. I wind the Victrola to life. And now the music scratchily plays throughout my cabin—and out upon my porch and over my trees and down through my valley and up into my mountains. Perhaps this music has waited all its life to be played here in a forest coronation. I cannot imagine a truer combination of the celestial and the earth-bound. I wish, Little Ones, you could hear the sound of such hope and splendor. That such a dignified creation by the hand of one man is attainable in this life. Alone as I am at this confluence of majesty and aspiration, of symphony and nature, and of divination and blessing, I cannot help but wish that you and your mother were here with me.

—Papa

Your Pappy's Love of Books and All Appearances of the Mother Tongue.

Dear Little Ones,

I AM DOOMED to read books.
If you haven't already figured it out, your pa can't
leave well enough alone, having to have my own last
word on books.

What a fine shake the gods have given you here. To
be born into a family of readers. To be amongst people
who believe that to be alive one must constantly keep
learning, both through the working of one's hands and
one's mind. I can remember quite a few times pounding
the fenceline far from headquarters, and somewhere in
the late and lazy afternoon scouting out a nice aspen or
Doug fir chairback, and catching a book break.

Why read, Little Ones?
Because it seems the world is most eagerly swan-
diving into the modern swamp of just-get-by perfection,
I'm-not responsible responsibility, and all the lying-truth
tapdances that we so eagerly use to perpetually reassure

ourselves that everything is good for us and that everything is okay, this illusion invading every aspect of our lives. Where the endless television endlessly promises more and more utterly useless bits of narcotic enlightenment, which are the cattle feed of our existence, fattening us up to be the perfect consuming consumers.

Because anything that smacks of originality or promise or hope is immediately seized upon as a ploy, a subterfuge, or some universal conspiracy that might wake us up and halt our downward dive, reminding us of what it is to feel, question, and, god forbid—think. And because thinking makes us think—how much more dangerous is that.

Yet what a magnificent hunger it is to read, Little Ones. To be aware that the more one learns, the more one appreciates one's own ignorance. Proving you are not afraid of knowledge or of changing how you look at the world. To be able to ask the timeless questions about salvation or free will—to god or not to god. Gathering up knowledge like cords of firewood, for the signal fire that must constantly burn hot and bright against the ever encroaching darkness of irrationality and ignorance.

Why read, Little Ones?

To think and to learn about who, what, and why we are. Books are written by mapmakers who endlessly illuminate, chart, and create the mind maps, and soul maps, and heart maps that we so need to help make sense of ourselves and our world. These explorers exist for one delectable prize and purpose—to define the beauty of contrarieties. To show us that we are not alone in our differences of how we ponder, savor, and believe—how we profess, and love, and die.

Somehow, in as many ways as these mapmakers individually perceive planets and earthworms, volcanoes and seashells, glaciers and dandelions, they eventually bring us to ourselves. Our individuality chooses to take the journey; our imagination chooses how we interpret these maps. And all these maps leading us to the pirate's treasure. And that treasure is ourselves.

Why read?

Because books are precious guides to our humanity—civilization's backbone—that tenuous ridgeline that allows us to climb above the jungle and see what the horizon has to offer. Thus they represent the yearning to go beyond, to explore. Yet they are also human-sized. And made of paper and ink, and thus they come from the earth. Their physicality is what makes them immensely human. And they contain the flesh-and-bone thoughts of one person capturing one blink of time, now made immortal in the bound pages carried by your own hands and touched by your own eyes. How can such fragile and thin paper and spidery veins of ink be our most precious treasure, binding together the entire hope and legacy and language of a civilization—of our existence. We touch the book and turn the page, and thus we are bound to our destiny.

Reading teaches us the nuances of humanity. To find the beauty of what is moral and ethical in your own actions and discover the strange subtlety of what it is to question why you should exist. And as you question what is within, so then will you question what is without, and you will bump headlong into all the others who are doing the same. This questioning and searching is the evolution of an individual who learns he or she must grow to stay strong. To consider the promise of transformation. To stay valuable to yourself. And to constantly learn—how amazing to be curious and curiouser and curiosity all in one.

General Patton once said, "If everyone is thinking alike, then someone isn't thinking." We need people in this world to think about consequences and actions. To understand what must be black and white, and to consider and imagine the certainties of what is gray—knowing that the interplay between shadows and light allows them both to stand together yet also to be distinct from one another. Be aware to this world, Little Ones. It is more magnificent than it is not. Seek the best from it. And become the best because of it. Listen. Look. Read.

Love,
Papa

Listen to Your Pappy's Music

Evening, Little Ones,

I'M LISTENING to the Victrola again. But now it is night, and the plain-spoken elegance of a piano turns me into pure memory, as though thirty years were but a minute before—now grandpa, his massive back silhouetted against the gauze-yellow light of the lantern, murmurs gracious incantations as he winds up the magic music box, and as he steps away, Chopin begins to play on the cabin porch—glistening notes wending their way through the night forest, floating up and against the granite mountains, kicking off the man-madeness of wood and wire, vinyl and needle, now heavenbound and going home.

My god, Little Ones, how I love music. How do I convey such love to you both? —"That I cannot even write to you while this damnable music is playing and so I must stop this beautiful sound.

How all music saturates my senses. Replaces my soul. Grinds me into the earth and burns me a new body as I'm born again into nothing but music bone and music skin. And when I write the music and play the music, I dream I am being drenched with the electricity of notes and anti-notes, and I barely need to exist.

Now all word-brave and music-drunk, I am ready to bring you to this magnificent love of mine. Hoping that the very essence of your pa's love of music lives and breathes within these words before you—hoping that this love endures in your minds as something more than a fanciful relic of thoughts.

Little Ones,

Music. Tunneling right down into your core and soultime. Hep, sloppy, sexy, and cerebral. Chancy and hip-swinging like Elvis and your first teenage kiss. Cantankerous and bumpy like a Hank Williams, Senior—a country sound to sashay you and your honey down the back road to the ranch where you work and now make out. A last cigarette and memory, in breakups to Sinatra. It's all the same tearing and heartbreak. The missing and the kissing. And then you lay open any old Beatle tune and turn scarlet and indigo with your discovery, and now you stand statuesque as you own the rock-and-roll.

You are the music of your era. Like the Benny Goodman, the Glenn Miller, and God Bless America taking away all our "Bugle Boys" to the last and greatest war.

Chance to prance and turn hip to hip—the first of your man-and-woman lusting is born on that dance floor where so many have strutted and hungered before. Ask your granddad about the censored goodbyes, the billets-doux, the Second Front, the Corregidor, and the madness and the eternal wait to never, and always, get back home.

Then there was sinless rock-and-roll that was blues shorn down to a white civility and all packaged up ready for the new generation of love makers. Buddy Holly, The Big Bopper, Little Richard. Innocent sex. And then rock-n-roll turned a threshold and became the words and ideas. Dylan. Baez. The Beatles. Melody and mayhem, and the country knew it was growing and the pains were evident in the song, and Camelot departed, and boys were a-dying somewhere bad where the young should never die but did. And we learned. The hardest way imaginable. And the music played on.

And whoa, boy, when you become the jazz and turn-spin to improv and smoke kiss; the choice tempo found between the two-drink minimum of ice-crackled vodka and the lovely purr of the alto sax cruising through your brain cells. Here you will discover the colloquy and the musings, all erring on the side of some 6\5 time that you could never beat out on your steering wheel but nonetheless know to be scorching every part of you and your growing intellect. Tasty from the start of the epoch. The Duke Ellington, the Count Basie, and through and on to all and every jazz I'll ever know and still dig.

Then there are the blues. Home-grown from Americana and slavery and crucifixion, all entitled to a special brand of excess and misery. But to follow the 12 bars into your agony, you must listen with nowhere to go, and mishap and love heavy on your mind. It is the quintessential experience of sorrow and sex. Blues, floating in from the Africa to the plantation, to the Man above and the man below. That changgey hurting blues harp sailing right through the middle of all that you thought you were. The grindey top-ended Fender Strat holding on to the last scream of a note longer than you thought imaginable, and you can't wish it to stop because it makes you cry and it makes you want and desire all that you can't have. And you wish there and then that nobody had ever invented that damn blues music, for it hurts you and caresses you like the best of love and woman that you have ever known.

And when your body and mind acquiesce to the timelessness of music, then you are ready to be born into the Classical. To be baptized by the sparkle-shine and innocence of Mozart and Haydn where the joyful dance can never end. To seek refuge in the exquisite order of Bach where benediction is so God-sent into every note, and you have no doubt that God must exist. To yield to the incessancy and aching of Rachmaninoff, giant hands plowing up notes from the piano, your heart beating mad and ferocious and crazy and desirous, stirring up your every saint and devil heartbeat to collide with each other. And then to fall revealed to Beethoven and his wracking magnificence, as he rebels against and impales himself upon his God in ceaseless tragedy and transcendence. And all this music of why God must take you, and of why you must go, will stab through all your veils of deceit. All this music, angel-born and salve-laden, will protect you with its innocence and joy. And the alchemy of notes and emotion will fill your soul with the inexpressible. Like some continual moment of revelation that must never end.

Such riches of music to listen to. Such beauty and sadness. How amazing to have this whole rapture ahead of you. As when you hear Gershwin's "Rhapsody in Blue" and can forget everything and become the music. And this is the improbable magic. Like a big train trip to the wild west. Like shaking apple tree blossoms into your hair. Like a succulent summer kiss. Such an ecstatic mystery and so elusive to the written word. Yet unless we are swaying to the dance, or following the notes, or creating the song, then I must fly here between the nonsense and the fervor of my words, in hopes that you will understand what can only and genuinely be heard with the heart and listened to with the ears.

Papa

The Losing of Love

Dear Little Ones,

WHAT A PRETTY EVENING. A little bit of God sprinkled everywhere.

I feel the odd tingle of cool air skimmering around the porch, brushing up against me like the angelic tickling of cattail feathers (that's what ma called them, showing me the delight of how to pull apart and free the thousands of "feather" flowers on the brown cattail stalk and then watch as the wind spun them all over the far and wide).

Little Ones, I wish you could smell this most intoxicating musk-and-myrrh of rain- saturated dirt, bark, stone, and sky that surrounds me. Like the smell of horse riding in early-morning autumn, and baby sleeping quietly amidst patchwork quilts, and pipe smoking around a wood stove during Christmas time. A smell with a small hint of impending sadness and somewhere a deep layer of tranquility.

I wish I could make the smell a color because how else do you describe the aliveness of rained-upon earth and god, stars and trees, except maybe to describe it as a color. An impossible color. Or maybe a color that doesn't exist. And in trying to describe it, you have to fail. Yet perhaps the failing is the color—the urgency, the wanting—of how much we voraciously desire to crawl inside this very moment, capture its every unbridled and tantalizing atom, and then somehow deliver it intact to another soul before the moment vanishes. Like discovering a shard of heaven's handwriting in the snowflake that has landed upon your hand, desperately wishing you could give such beauty to your best friend before it melts away. And what you are left with is an exquisite regret—the eloquent conspiracy of memory—of the moment lived and the moment wished for that never will arrive.

Maybe, Little Ones, this is how I needed to arrive to the losing of love. Through this rain drenching, and color that can't be, and snowflakes that must melt. Through moments lived and moments hauntingly wished for. For this most certainly is love, and love's death.

Little Ones,

So many loves to lose, in so many ways. The promise of a magnificent ideal that somehow becomes tainted, tarnished, or broken. The devotion of a great friendship that somehow becomes a betrayal of trust. The unquestioning companionship that was the love of a long-time pet now gone. The once bright passion of newlyweds slowly dulled by time, their love imperceptibly carried away by a thousand million waves of conformity and routine, until love is fatefully washed away. But the profound loves, that for which you would give most anything to and sacrifice most everything for, are the most painful of all to lose— the parent or child, the brother or sister, the husband or wife, the friend or the lover.

The first losing of love is usually your heart. And the trueness and beauty of the first time you love most often belongs to a young heart. One that only knows the falling into love, never imagining its loss. For no one can tell you—prepare you—for the absence, disappearance, minus-ness, nothingness, limbo, and void of losing love. How does one imagine joy and happiness suddenly freezing and shattering like ice-frosted rose petals to then be maliciously strewn and scattered by every wind, real and imagined. You feel an exquisite breaking pain like no other pain in the world, and you know your heart has lost, for a time, its purpose, and that purpose was to love.

Losing a heart's love feels like having your head cut off over and over again. You think your world is coming to an end at least ten times a day. And it is. No doubt about it. If people tell you that someday you'll get over it or that there are more fish in the sea, tell them to go suck on a cactus—you won't get over it and there are no more fish in the sea. The only antidote is time.

The only real help for such a loss is having the most magnificent friends in the whole of the oceans and continents and seas stand by you as you cry and blubber and wail yourself into a state of idiocy, listen to you repeat the same lament for the forty-forth and seventy-first and one-hundredth and fifty-sixth time, prevent you from putting your fist through immobile objects like walls and trees, and make sure you don't drink yourself to a standstill. They are just there to be with you—whenever and however you may need them.

And if you have no one to hold onto, then you must find someone. For this love wanting is the falling dream where you never hit bottom but fall and fall and fall—a most awful nowhereness in which to be alone. You should not have to endure such pain by yourself, for we are alone enough in our skins and souls as it is. And you will tear yourself up with the sharpest claws of your being. And your heart will be truly and wickedly wounded in this battle and battlefield you thought could never exist.

The second losing of love is forever, and this forever is death. And I will tell you, Little Ones, that losing this love can not only break your heart, but can murder your thoughts and shatter your soul. And whether one meets the loss slowly, as through an illness, or is shocked into nothingness by an inconceivable god-gone accident, or receives the impersonal and sanitized communiqué of a loved one lost in war, the foreverness is what torments you. That all possibility to say what must be said, feel what must be felt, love how one must love, is now the forever of never—that is what no one can comprehend until one loses such a love.

No one is quite certain how long this death will last within you before you find your way back into life. No one can tell you when you should be finished. No one can decide for you. For no one, but no one, can see into the dungeon of your pain except you. You must feel as you do until you decide you are done feeling this way. And your death may last a very long time. Yet, eventually and hopefully and somehow, you will be able to return to yourself. Each step will seem like a first step. You will gradually begin to see and to breathe again. You will find that you can talk and maybe even smile. And a smile will beget a laugh. Like a lamb once lost in the dark hills and woods, you will find yourself welcomed back into the fold of this world. And maybe someday, with hope to befriend you and faith to guide you, you will find life—and love—again.

Yet sometimes such a losing of love is a death that will never leave you. And maybe this aching cannot end, for it will burn inside you like some cruel and relentless ember which sears into your very bones and marrow. You will dream of this love during the smallest fragments of your day, which is a minefield of memory. You will dream of this love during the longest of your echoing nights, which contain the merry-go-round of your greatest fears and longings. And the dreaming never seems to end. Until the wounding within you becomes the ghost that you must live with. And when this ghost becomes entwined within your very soul, it will then be a ghost no longer. It has dissolved into you. It is now the memory in your walk and breath, the passion behind a grail sought for and never quite found, and there is nothing that God or you can do to change this. And when you understand that it is possible for someone you have lost to become part of who you are, only then will you realize a most amazing and different life, filled with an immense power and sadness, so infinitely unexplainable and yet so ferocious with purpose.

I am sorry that this life you live will embody such immensity and complexity of suffering. Yet in the guise of the terrible you will gain a wisdom and humility you have never known. You will be changed by an unwilled scar upon your heart where there was none before. And that scar is a reminder to you for all time. You will realize, in the deepest realm of where your knowing and your heart collide, that a fragment of heaven fell to you, and forever became part of you. You will understand so very clearly the chasm between earth and heaven. Between what is merely living and knowing what it is to be alive. And in this way, you are changed forever. Forever.

—Papa

August 13

1:40 a.m.

I WAKE UP. The moon is still out. I look at it through my window, from my warm bed, and see the first telltale cold crystals of fall upon the window panes.

I get up and walk the night fields. The first harbinger frost has come to the mountains, clinging to the bunch grass, and I can hear my boots crunching upon it. The moon is near full, so quiet and silver-white. It hangs there—magical, fat, and contented. This is another moment, a good moment. They will come and then go, but for now I am here. And there is no other place I can be—nor need to be. The frost has taken on an alpine glow. A sheen of crystalline blue and white lies over the land.

I think of my leaving all of this. I don't want to. Not unless there is more of the same on the other side. If there are no mountains or fields or moonlight… I will not go.

I am writing this to you because—I'm not exactly sure. There's no lesson to be taught here. No practical this or that. No morality. I guess I want you to know how much I want to live. I want you to know the man, not just the father. For one moment.

There is a part of me that knows how to die. With dignity. With grace. I don't want to do it in bed—that's for damn sure. I can do it alone, if that's what it takes. I would rather do it dying for a cause—for my kin, my wife and children; for my country; for the grand and moral ideas that are worth dying for. These are the best reasons to die.

I would rather live. Up to whatever last moment is given to me. Awake and kicking hard to stay out of the last great beyond. I am a fighter. I want all the suffering and joy and beauty and tears that life can throw at me. I don't want cosmic peace and understanding. I don't want universal acceptance and everlasting happiness. Don't want them. I want the glory of imperfection. The art of being human. It's the trying to make it work that so enchants me about living. It is the damnedest of heartache and sorrow. It is the pinnacle of laughter and happiness. And everything that's in between.

So, death, I say kiss off. And if you're looking for a good brawl, then I'm ready. I have no fear of you. Only a fear of not loving and living deeply enough. And I'm not ready to go, whatever plans you may have to the contrary. You've chosen a man who is still alive, knows who he is, and knows what he wants in this world. This is a dangerous man. I do not feel in a Zen mood. I do not feel in an accepting mood. You definitely haven't chosen a saint. I've seen the good and the bad, and have been a bit of both. So, I'm not exactly gearing up to get into heaven, nor do I have any inclination toward trudging off to hell. You're determined to take this man off his land and he doesn't want to go.

You haven't seen a thing until you've seen this man fight. My sword is sharp. My heart strong. My spirit ferocious—and I am going to live. Let the swords clash. Let the fight begin.

August 17

5:32 a.m.

Little Ones,

MORNING. Cut out in vast blocks of green and blue. Feather-light. Arriving like fresh spring water. All burbly and clear, not quite sure where the going is, but at least there is a going. Newborn. Like a pretty bay colt, just foaled and all fired up about being all fired up. Morning. Plain and pretty. Like a pretty girl in a pretty dress going to a barn dance, young, with a turn and a kilting to her walk. Smiling with the promise of a hidden kiss to be offered to the man of her dreams, but he doesn't know it yet.

Your mother. When we would wake, early in the early, just at earth's turning, the first words spoken were no words at all. Only a look. Into each other, as we held each other. Every morning seemingly the first and the last. In wonder that the day was still born from night, and that emerging from the shadowland of dreams, we always woke safely to each other's arms.

The cow elk are feeding just a field and some beyond the cabin. Speckled brown against the tall grama grass of the meadow. Such a fine morning. A promise and hope of a morning. Possibly with a miracle waiting around the corner. Someone once said that where exists a great love there are always miracles. I have to believe that. But you should know that your old man is the biggest, most hopeful and sentimental, fool of them all. Such a fool that he believes in hope and beauty, faith and love. Even when all else seems hardscrabble and crestfallen. You two are the first miracles to arrive from a great love. I think your mother will agree. The miracles will not stop. This much I know.

I have come to a habit now. As I awake I greet you and your mother with a good morning. I imagine what it would be like to say such words to your mother again, and to say such words to you for the first time. You are in my waking and in my going to sleep. The simple words I write bring you beside me. It may seem silly that I say such things, but only silly like a love. And that is what I have for you, and you.

Good Morning.

Papa

The Everything and Nothing of Money

Good Morning again, Little Ones,

Y OUR PA AND MONEY. Like dancing porcupines crashing a balloon party—not a felicitous mix. Always with a thistly sense that money and I were never going to be two Rockefellers cavorting together on the back porch, smoking delectably-aged Cubans and reveling in our business savvy and grand fortune. I've noticed over the years, Little Ones, that certain people and money seem to fit together as when a smart horse knows it's being ridden by a smart rider, and horse, rider, and saddle all become one. But your pa, being born with a good dose of the contrary, never saw fit to make cozy with money, let alone be able to ride it with ease and command. For money, as far as your pa is concerned, is every god-sin-devil-pleasure-necessity-desire, greed-lust-dragon-scorching, evil-grubbing, hallelujah-hugging, yee-haw-life-is-good contradiction known to man. And that's as simply as your pa can begin to put it.

Little Ones,

The everything and nothing of money is...

You need it like air. You want it like whiskey. Sometimes you even desire it like the desiring of a love or a person—but can't have it. You can't live without it, and you're always looking for a way to find more. Too much can make you happily unhappy. Too little can make you habitually unhappy. But finding the happy middle is like trying to balance a cube of Jell-O on the end of your fingertip.

Money. It fits around your neck like some permanent noose, always waiting for your next misstep. It's angel wine, of which one sip will send you into ecstatic deliriums and roaring enchantments. It can reduce a man to a crying idiot, encircling and ensnaring him in a Gordian knot of financial spiderwebs.

Money. It makes people crazy with a generosity that defies gravity and is beyond explanation. It makes others, as gramps would say, so stingy they wouldn't pay a dime to see an earthquake. And by hook, crook, fancy and delancy, it makes people lie, cheat, steal, blackmail, extort, defame, murder, swindle, and even call each other bad names.

Money. While in the throes of love, it can warp your best intentions (because if you think you can buy love, your're both right and wrong). While in the midst of marriage, it can sink the ship or send it sailing on its merry way. Without it, governments would crumble like sandcastles, and wars would ever be wanting.

Money. It makes people thing-crazy. Want, want, want. More, more, more. Without it, you don't eat. With it, we learn to lust—for the next want we don't need, but know we can have. It's envy always in your back pocket. It deludes people into believing that money makes them better than other people, for it's the beggar's soap that makes all men smell rich

Money. It feeds your finest vices as a devil at the ready. It's one of the greatest aphrodisiacs, feeding the lust-fury of the rich and powerful, and one of the most potent depressants, pounding in hammer-and-sledge profusion the spirits of those who go without. It's the great laughter-killer and the gorgeous instant gratifier.

And not a day goes by that we're not working for it, dying because of it, anxious over lack of it, planning futures because of it, buying because we have it, compromising our health, love, and security because we have so little of it, and ever and always thinking about it until the last moment of our mazely lives.

Well, Little Ones, now that your old man has completely mystified and bambaffled you about the what and wherefores of money, it's time to drag the eternal five-thousand pound bull into the china shop of our questioning—can money buy you happiness? And the real heart and soul and contradiction of money is both yes and no.

But more importantly in my book of life, it's what you can't buy with money that is often more important than what you can buy.

Can money buy you a house? Of course, but it cannot make you a home. It can buy you a friend but never friendship—this has to be earned. It can buy you a person's obligation but never his loyalty. It can make you put up with your work, but never make you love it. You can buy power with money but never respect. It can buy you pills galore, but it can't buy you true health.

Money—it can buy you a moment of glee but not a lifetime of happiness. It can buy you a diamond ring but not a great marriage. It can buy your kids anything, but it cannot teach them love, respect, and the true value of living life without things. Yes, money can buy you knowledge, but not the wisdom to use it wisely. It can buy you a ticket to travel, but not the curiosity to discover the world you're traveling through.

Money cannot buy desert sunsets, the giggle of a baby, the sweetness in autumn corn, a perfectly thrown touchdown pass, a warming sun on an ice-cold day, believing in Santa Claus, or a first kiss. It cannot buy you a great conversation nor the memory of a perfect moment. It cannot buy your watching in silence the delicate walk of a fawn as it follows its mother through the pines. It cannot buy the exact moment when your little one says papa or mama to you.

Money cannot buy you faith in yourself, others, or God. It cannot buy courage—of any kind. It cannot buy you honesty of thought or action, the conviction of your ideas, nor the determination to endure in any contest or endeavor.

Money may buy you the means to a happiness, but it cannot buy happiness itself.

But, Papa, you really can't live without money. And yes, you are right, Little Ones. You need money to live. And that's when we buy for necessity—to put food on the table and to clothe our families, and to make sure there is the shelter of our house. To make sure we can pay the doctor when we are sick and the mechanic when the car has broken down. And to make sure we have light and water, which are so determinedly essential to all life that I can't imagine not having enough money to assure their daily existence. All these basics are the most important and rightful use of money. And god only knows, when you can't pay the bills, money becomes like a canteen of precious water in an endless sandstorm.

And, Papa, not every thing you buy has to be a necessity. And yes, you are right again, Little Ones. But it is the quality of a thing rather than the quantity of things that your papa is concerned with. And your old man's philosophical yardstick for the acquisition of a thing is threefold: does it have thoughtfulness, purpose, and perhaps even beauty? And why not all three? Finding a fine-fit saddle or a good working horse. Discovering a hard-back book (to which your pa is partial), or a nice piece of china for your mom. Who doesn't enjoy the pride of ownership when you have sacrificed to buy something special and that something has both meaning and purpose, when someday it might embody the history of its owner, and even find its way into the family legacy. Or it can help the creation of some grand memory as when your mother and I hoofed in it down through that geologic mural of earth's history, to the very bottom of the Grand Canyon, or spent weeks motoring up that magnificent blueline of Highway 1, gazing out at the Pacific at all hours of the day and night. Lastly, a some-thing should invite a sense of purposeful happiness rather than the sparkle-eyed covetous spasm of "mine-mine-mine" self-gratification that is the working mantra for all toddlers, whose rightful sense of ownership is defined in fractions of child minutes, or possibly of baby seconds.

Yet look around you, Little Ones. You would think we live by the credo, "the more, the merrier—a lot more, the more merrier." And, if this were actually true, then there should be endless flocks of people running around happy as larks in a flitting contest. Or maybe a better buying battle cry would be, "Enough is never enough, and a little is always too little!"

So how much of a thing or things is enough? And if you have everything, have you achieved perfect happiness? What a strange end to that argument. Or is enough never enough—and much like the drunk forever chasing after the next drink to put the next smile on his face, and the next smile after the next smile, you'll always need one more drink and—you get the picture. Or as grandpa would picturesquely remind me upon discovering another example of the intricacy of human folly at work, "like blind men trying to catch oiled eels."

Now why, do you ask, is this philosophizing about money and the buying of things so hell-fired important. Because, Little Ones, your papa believes that what you have to watch out for in this life is when you can't tell whether you're living your life or buying your life. When you're working so hard for the next thing to acquire, you soon forget that instead of you owning your things, they begin to own you—that buying just to buy is just living from one thing to another thing. And by being in hock to things—and more things and more things—which somehow and supposedly make us happier, we are forced to work longer and harder to not only keep the things we already have but to also get even more things—and we end up squandering the greatest currency of our lives—time—for things. Is this cockamamie or what?

So, if the truest currency of life is time, then how do you get more time? Because if more is merrier, than having more time should make us more happier. Right? Therefore, all we have to ask ourselves is can we buy more time?

And the royal answer is:

No. And more no. And forever no.

Money can buy you everything to fill your time but it cannot buy time itself. And things are definitely not time.

In the beginning, you are given a lump sum of time, and every hour lived is an hour spent. No getting a life loan to buy another year. No asking for more credit to purchase a few more days. No borrowing from your buddy a few bucks to buy a few more hours.

And in the end, are we remembered for what we bought, or for the quality of the time we spent in living? Are we remembered for how tightly we chained ourselves to the workwheel, or for the person we were with our families and friends, what we did for others and how true we were to ourselves and the life we led—not just for what we did with our lives, but how we did it? Because I'll tell you right now, Little Ones, when push comes to shove, no one's asking to work another hour to buy another some-thing while tossing around on their deathsheets.

From where your papa sits, watching as the bank account of my time dwindles away much faster than I had anticipated or appreciate, I'm not asking you to take vows of poverty but vows of deliberation. For things don't think, and money has no mind. Only you can know the difference between your wants and your needs, and the sacrifice of your life's time to both.

Remember, Little Ones, everything is not important all the time. Only living is important all the time. Not things. Not money. Not more things and more endless money. Spend well the quality of your time. And yes, be greedy with your hours. If only to then give those hours away as the most precious gifts you have to offer to yourself, your family, and your friends. And yes, to my Little Ones.

Love,
Papa

August 22
5:02 a.m.

I remember.

FOG. ALMOST EVERYWHERE. Like awakening from a long dream, though not quite sure of what you dreamt. An ocean morning, still star-laden. Where cottage windows, opened to allow the night air, also invited in the cloak of Calais fog. Each wave against the shore so exactly pitch-perfect, each crescendo upon the rocks like a new-sworn vow. Therein lay the flawless comfort. Knowing that a million more waves in time would each make their morning call—whether or not we were there.

I can still picture so clearly your mother beside me in the weightless light before the sun arrived. Curled up against me. Safe next to my warmth. Often, in her sleep, I would gently caress her hair. So slowly. In time with each wave. And she would not awaken. Yet her breath would slow and whatever anxiousness the night had brought would dissipate beneath my touch. I never grew tired of waking up beside her. Of feeling her body nudge up next to mine in some morning ritual that seemed so timeless. As if this lifetime, never-ending, could only lead to many more. Her hair so dark against the snowdust-white of the pillows. Her small body lost under a sea of ivory-quilted down. Each moment together, complete. As if we had never known a being apart. Such a forever feeling that my words break and dissolve at the edge of their ability to define.

I can smell the strong salt air. I can hear the distant bellow of the fog horn buoy. I can see through the velvet dimness of this morning, dark and light. I can feel her next to me. This union. Of warmth. Of caring. Of the indescribable. As if there were no parting and never could be. So, silently, goes this dawning. This is how I loved, and love, your mother.

To Make a Marriage Live or Die

Dear Little Ones,

As I sit here upon the porch, watching this morning unfold like a meadow prayer, I wonder at the machinery of marriage—all those unseen gears, pulleys, ratchets, and spindles—somehow moving two people forward in both awkward and elegant unison, toward endless and ever-changing destinations. And how, when that machinery slowly breaks down—so gradually, like the grains of sand crumbling off of an old sand castle— we slowly move apart, until the breaking is all that is left of marriage. And how it doesn't have to be that way.

Perhaps this is one of the most difficult letters of all to write. Pointing the tip of my pen at this most vulnerable jugular of my thoughts—the marriage of your mother and me. Sometimes I wonder—strangely wonder—what if I had learned to die sooner, would I have somehow made a better husband—and been truly better if I had lived.

Now Little Ones, I must make a new spring from old summer fires. Where the pines and flowers demand to grow from the scorched earth, and to flourish again. And now as I write to you both, I must make wisdom from my mistakes, find grace in my undoing. And this wisdom must become a wish—for you both to find a love requited, that which endures beyond the constant and earthbound hardship, one that seeks to discover every small and great celebration possible, both sacred and familiar, intimate and contented, a love endlessly forgiving and somehow lasting forever—and to call this wish your marriage.

Little Ones, as I see it, you get married—but you make a marriage. Some folks think that, once they're married, they've already arrived in Paris, where you drink chilled wine in picnic-in-the-park afternoons, and somehow evening roses bewitchingly appear by the bedside, and you step feather-heeled, strolling through dusky and swoon-filled romantic nights, and... and somehow you forget that to get to Paris you have to travel to Paris. Marriage is not the beginning of the journey, nor the end—it is the journey. Where you decided by some magical and incandescent flicker of the flame that the journey of life was made somehow better, deeper, richer, more fulfilling by experiencing it with someone else. And that making sure that the magic never wanes and the flame never dies is your most important responsibility to each other.

But the strangest thing happens on the way to making a marriage. The romance begins to rust. The love loses its luster. The friendship flounders and the magic becomes musty. What happened? You expected Casablanca and you got the Honeymooners. Somehow and somewhere in our foolish quest for a forever love, we forget that for silver to shine you have to constantly polish it. And when you don't, the silver tarnishes.

Marriage is love put to its ultimate test—the grindstone of life. Where the idealism of love meets the everydayness of marriage. Yes, you started out simply as each other's lover, companion, and friend, but now you are a couple, a corporation, a legal entity, an island unto yourselves, a family, a social grouping, a mister and missus, and two peas in a pod. You are also now the breadwinner, the babymaker and sitter, the maintenance worker, the repairman, the short-order cook, the financial analyst and bookkeeper, the medical staff, the mechanic, and the gardener. You are the teacher, taxi driver, sanitation worker, spiritual advisor, vacation planner, son-in-law/daughter-in-law, mother, father, aunt, uncle—did I miss anything? And you wonder why the lightness of love becomes the elephant of resentment, inexorably stomping up your backside to someday establish a permanent perch.

How do you make a marriage die? Slowly. Very slowly. So slowly that even watching the moon make its way across the night sky seems like a drag race. If you don't think that love can slowly die, then you are a romantic steeped in the starry-eyed, love-never-fails endings of love-is-forever sonnets and novels, and doomed to watch Wuthering Heights reruns like an endless and tragedy-addicted love zombie. A marriage dying dies a thousand thousand intimate and tiny deaths, all very very slowly and all mostly invisible.

And you may rightfully ask yourselves, why on earth is your pa talking about the death of marriage before he talks about what makes a marriage great? Because, Little Ones, as I realize in my grasping to comprehend the past, when you finally realize a marriage is truly dying, it's usually too late to revive it. Not always, but usually.

And what causes it to die?

Two people.

Because it takes two to tango.

Otherwise, it's not a tango.

Otherwise, it's not a marriage.

To make a marriage die is simple. To make a marriage live is work.

The less you work at it, the simpler it gets. Until you are only married on paper and little else.

And how do you do it—that is, make a marriage die: Where once you expected your Prince Charming and your Cinderella to somehow retain their magical allures, irresistible courtesies, and engaging sincerities, you are supremely mortified when they begin to chew food like some greedy banana-grubbing gorilla, or start to leave their clothes strewn across the vast swaths of the house like giant breadcrumbs dropped in the forest, or commence to bark out directives like a born-to-the-task whip-cracker, or slowly shackle all your associations with your friends with a perdition's list of household tasks, or just maybe play the perfect Jekyll-and-Hyde card on you as they become the exact-and-opposite person from the one you thought you married. And thus slowly the weather of time peels away the mask of courtship paint, only to reveal the real person you really married.

Where once you talked like living encyclopedias, you have gradually begun to communicate through the marriage Morse code of semi-finished thoughts and grunted yesses and nos. Each day, by incrementally building the most intricate and flawlessly constructed walls and tunnels to what you can or cannot talk about, you manufacture the perfect maze of artificial tranquility from which you can never find your way out. And thus you slowly and most assuredly trap your way out of understanding and love.

Where once there were two of you and the world was right and bright and full of firemaking, there are now three or four or five of you—and now with children you're slowly learning a brand-new definition of romance as your time together, as a couple, has been reduced to the possibility of making passionate sleep, and maybe actually sleeping. Now the two of you have become a house of mirrors, multiplied into professional everyones and everythings, exhaustively maintaining, watching, securing, guiding, and balancing a universe of house and family, and friends, and work, and life and—and in the sliver of twilight, before you close your eyes for the night, you wonder why the flame of love and affection and desire and romance flickers like a dying candle aching for another moment of oxygen to stay alive and lit.

Where now just beyond the babies are the bills and the business of running a marriage. Money. The third person lurking in your bed. The calculating mistress in your head. The bogeyman hiding in your checkbook. Money, the poison pill of power, slowly turning you into the tempter, the finagler, the con man, and the shrew. Money, forcing the trinity of your marriage—love, trust, and respect—into a game of Russian roulette poker, played with wicked jackals, lazy Satans, and really abominable snowmen. And the slow-motion pity and accident of it all is when you realize how effortlessly the kingdom of money can eventually replace the intimacy of love.

Where, of course, you've never had a cross word, or god forbid a fight—until the first one. And unless you know how to properly fight in a marriage, everyone wants to win, and thus everyone loses. Which inevitably leads to a second fight, which then leads to an argument, and then another fight. And always the bull's-eye of your resentment, anger, or annoyance is fortunately near at hand, an opportunistic target you'll rarely miss. And what do you fight about? In a marriage, everything and nothing. Petty, pick-a-fight irritations, justifiable misunderstandings, at-that-moment botherations. Of course, kids—manners, disciplining, teaching, and everything else about them. Not talking with your spouse. Bills paid and unpaid and that never will be paid. Christmas at whose house? Thanksgiving where? How do we afford this? Needy relatives, trying friends, annoying co-workers. Procrastination, laziness, slothfulness and all manner of grand and small faults, foibles, and vices. And in a thousand thousand tussles over many many years, you'll bicker, snipe, squabble, feud, battle, brawl until—like the single-minded persistence of ants upon a carcass—you've picked clean the bones of what was once a love and patience between two people.

And where thank-yous once flourished like baby smiles, and caresses tumbled down upon you like snowflakes in love, and gestures of gratitude abounded like magic poems that suddenly appeared out of nowhere, you now take for granted the warmth of your boredom and routine, living in the constant history of a love that once was, having long-ago and sincerely suffocated the last remnants of all appreciation and gratitude.

So many ways and more that a marriage can die. And you wonder why people get married?

Yet, the many ways that it can die, are the many ways that it can live.

Because, Little Ones, like the mixing of light and stars, sunshine and flowers, and children and curiosity, when marriage is mixed together in proper proportion and through perfect mystifying alchemy—the gargantuan weight of the universe can be upheld by the sheer tenacity and lightness of two people who understand the infinite variations of constantly falling in love over and over again.

But falling in love over and over again takes work. And constant vigilance. And fine tuning. And more work. You must want to love each other over and over again. And find every way imaginable to make that happen. Otherwise, the sheer gravity of time and toil will inevitably force love to fade, and what once was a willing and wanting union of love and life becomes the thinning and ancient parchment of a paper marriage—and that is not love, and that cannot be love.

Now, Little Ones, I must stop for the morning to rest this tired mind. To wash myself of the mud of melancholy and disappointment. Of history. And to remember why love truly and always desires to be kept alive.

Papa

Night

Little Ones,

LOOK AT THE STARS. Everywhere. Gilded by the half-crescent waxing of a Shakespearean moon. Vapory tongues of black-currant clouds encircling and releasing every constellation. A Shangri-la night would taste like this.

I am at meadow's edge on some haunting old deer path deep in the wane of night. So silent except for the sandpaper scritching of my pen on glimmering silver-lit paper. And sovereign moon dust is sprinkled over man and earth.

My cabin. Lit up like a small bit of Halloween. Orange-brimmed and yellow curtain-called. So tiny an anchor. This wooden lightship that carries the crooked pain and penance of one man.

All thoughts and times are ceasing before my eyes. Perhaps I will make a bed of pine boughs and sage tonight. And if night should amaze me and go on forever, then I will go with it. And put to sleep all betrayals and debts.

August 27

9:22 p.m.
warm and starry

Dear Little Ones,

T HIS IS HOW I WANT to remember...

Summer, dropping so easily a delicious everything upon your skin and lips. Like a never-ending kiss—taunting, deep, and luscious. The sun. The heat. The thousand echoes of a timelessness before time, when every day seems longer than the next and no day seems likely to ever truly end. Summer. The only and best time. Those in-between years when you can't get old enough quick enough, and you have no idea that you are the perfect age. The just-before time. The just-before the necessary job. The just-before marriage and children. The just-before, when soon you must accept all decisions as your sole responsibility. And there is still a chance to be as wondrous as an Arabian dream, daring and wanting. A dream that snaps like hot sand under your feet; and the oasis, the myrrh and the gold are yours for the taking.

A pure time. Not knowing where you are going and not giving a bother or a damn. That volcano-time of urge and jungle aching, with a voodoo desire for all that is possible to a man and woman. Your tanned skin blued by the cooling lake, and everywhere there exists a craving for a stolen caress, innocent and intentional, and always the signal is understood. You are the body. Strong, muscular. The grand temptation of youth and energy harnessed to an animal engine that roars and purrs with every breath you take. God, you are perfect. The bliss of youth. And all around you is a new and unknown world, dovetailed and flawed and scary as all hell, and you give a damn and you don't give a damn, and thus you are fearless. Fearless, perfect, and endless. For nothing has been written in stone. Nothing. All is possibility.

Summer, and you are the first car of youth that tastes the finest freedom you've ever known, shining like blue-jet, burning like rocket fuel, ready to break the sound barrier for nothing and a dare. You are the music that careens out of every nook of radio and stereo, bathing you in the armor of independence, casting over you such a serious enchantment that you become the source of all lyrics you hear. Each word speaks to you so honestly that you feel you are the only poet that should be allowed to exist, for you understand the music so perfectly.

Summer, and you are the first man and the first woman to kiss. The first to know the exacting, steel-ing pain of a broken heart. The first to know everything about the whole cascading universe of gods and stars and lunacy and tenderness. Thus you become the first man and woman to know love. And God help you, for you are now the first man and woman in the world.

And the sun, in all this prattle of knowing and unknowing, must soon surrender to a slow exit and assume its distant duty. Now there is twilight. When the mountain and the pine and the perfect day simmer to an incense that lie lushly upon you. Where one hand folds gently into another. And you commit the first circle of a myriad summers to memory. Of the desire and the hunt and the realization. And then there is the last moment. An absolute amidst this cooling heat. With cricket song. And the graciousness of night. The blessing of a midsummer's night dream. Inhabited by the most flawless seconds imaginable, between the roar and the calm of your steadfast heart. And the enduring day continues into the enduring night. And the possibilities are endless.

Have a good autumn morning

Greeting, Little Joe,

You have some things I want to leave... Old envy... They are English history of what... what I loved. They are energies for my... to told — for your hangs to told. There things... mostly important to me. They might becom... important to you.

When I got ready to go, I'll leave the... with the letters.

My guitar. Tell you... many to care you... if I secured a place right up front for you... When it's okay, age, the guitar will be simple...

Fall...

September 1

Hoot owls and autumn arriving

Evening, Little Ones,

I HAVE SOME THINGS I WANT to leave you both. They are small histories of who your old man was—of how I believed, and of who and what I loved. They are memories for my hands to hold—for your hands to hold. These things are mostly important to me. They might become important to you.

When I get ready to go, I'll leave them with the letters.

My guitar. Tell your mamma to carve your names on it. I reserved a place right up front for you two. When she's done, the guitar will be complete.

My U.S. flag. I always carry it with me when I'm on the road or at home. Your great-grandpa gave it to me, so it doesn't have all fifty stars on it. Remember to fold it with the blue side up.

My work gloves from stringing a certain barbed wire fence years ago.

My Uncle Henry pocketknife I always keep with me. My first pair of Paul Bond boots. The big hole in the side was where one of Grandpa's bulls decided to use me as a pincushion.

Some of the drawings I sketched for your mom when we climbed Saddle Mountain years ago. That's where I proposed to her. Make sure your mom gets them back.

My little black atlas I've always had. I was trying to keep up with the world but all the countries kept changing and that's why it's so marked up. All the places I've always wanted to go to are marked in red. Maybe you'll get there someday.

A half-melted pocket watch that Peachy Scottysworth gave me as a souvenir from that big fire we fought up in Montana. We ran like greyhounds with our tails on fire. He lost the watch just before we dived into a creek. He went back and found it later, and then sent it on to me. When something got in his craw, he'd go to fulminating with "God's Holy Trousers" or "Devil Done Dammit." They don't make many like Peachy anymore.

My medicine bag with soil from the ranch, a few rattler tails, a crow's feather I've had since I was a kid, and some other knick-knack sacreds that I felt were important to carry with me throughout my life.

All the songs I've written to you during this time. My Bowie hunting knife. The one my folks gave me for making it through college.

A plain metal drinking cup with the name Butch

C carved on it. My ma gave it to me on my seventh birthday. She told me Butch Cassidy left it when he came by Grandpa's ranch way back in the olden days. Biggest darn thrill of my life. Still, it might have been some old cowboy who had nothing better to do than scratch names into old tin cups and pass them off as Cassidy's or Sundance's. I never asked Ma if the story was true or not, and she never said anything contrary-wise.

All the little inspirational and love notes your mom would leave for me to find down at the printing press when I had to work all night.

The little bronze horse she would somehow always tuck away in my saddlebags or suitcase when I wasn't looking, and which I would inevitably find when I was out in the field or on the road. It was our good luck horse.

My cigar box with some pictures of your mom and me when were up climbing around the Sawtooths. The gold is from a small claim I staked fourteen miles out of Dawson, up in the Yukon. That little nugget is my pride and joy. I call it Geronimo because it was hell to pull out of the creek's bedrock. And the bullet was taken from a buddy of mine who didn't make it through Korea. He told the medic to pass it on to me.

My Winchester 30-30 that my brothers bought for me as a going-away present.

A bottle of Jim Beam that Rod and I have been saving up for years. It's marked with all the dinners I ever had to buy him. We figured that whoever lived the longest would get one remarkable bottle of sipping whiskey. All the dates and places are where we had dinner. You see, we made an extra pact on the side that said each time one of us moved he had to buy the other one dinner. As you can see, Rod stay glued and I ended up buying all the dinners. Will you please pass this bottle on to him, Little Ones?

I've got two leather bridles with me. One is for Boots and the other is for Gracie. There aren't two better horses in the entire world. Your mom and I got married on them. I'm giving you Gracie's bridle. I think I'll take Boot's with me.

My rodeo buckle was given to me by Skiver Dan who rode a bucking horse like he was taking a walk-on-water stroll just for the fun of it. Eight seconds in heaven couldn't be any sweeter.

My black leather cigar carrier was especially made for me by your mom when I was just a young buck. She had it sized to hold those small Romeo y Julieta's I like so well. This and the buckle go everywhere with me.

My favorite pipe which my pa gave to me.
The family Bible which my ma gave me.
My writing pen.
And these words. To you.

Love,
Papa

September 2

6:02 a.m.

Toast Your Old Man and Remember the Seasons

Little Ones,

I WISH YOU BOTH could hear it—there—echoing off the mountain walls. Like an earth horn. As if the land were some strange musical instrument—the sound like a forgotten and earth-ancient lament that's been trapped underground for a thousand years, now resounding through miles and miles of rock, finally emerging as some unearthly song, so fiercely hypnotic, and it captures me stone-still. It is a haunting—the warring high-pitched cry of some young bull elk as he trumpets his challenge to the old bull for his kingdom and his harem—then antlers clash and splinter against one another—and so the primal gauntlet is endlessly and forever thrown down. —And this echo I have heard ever since I was a young boy, burned into my very bones—fall has arrived again. One last time.

I already miss fall, and it's barely begun. Maybe it's because the lazy memories of summer are over and now begins the real remembering. Where the perpetual memory of my youth still keenly watches as Grandpa points out the meteorology of the early-winter arrival of kestrels and marsh hawks hastily heading south, accompanied by the great flying arrowheads of Canadian Geese winging and honking their way through the fall-blue sky. And then Grandpa slyly philosophizes on the merits of being able to eat the house that one lives in while we observe Mr. Beaver, from the banks of the big pond, hauling in another cache of tasty cottonwood branches that will help to expand his winter lodge.

Grandpa called it the short goodbye—fall, that is. Like a Moses-cowboy, perched there atop his bay, seated in his Hamley like he'd been born to a saddle on his britches, and gazing out over his high-pasture dominion, he'd declare that every day of fall was a good day for living, and could be a damn good one for dying. And never comprehending a lick of what he was saying or seeing, and especially thinking, I'd stare out into his valley and up into his mountains, somehow knowing I was predestined to spend the rest of my short life trying to decipher what he meant.

And nothing has changed since I was a kid, for I still see from the porch the sharp red-orange of the autumn mountain ash berries far atop the rockfall. And most everywhere upon the hillsides, I can watch the turning of the aspens from summer-meadow green to their palatial gold-dipped yellow—like a light dance, shimmering so lusciously in the sunlight it almost hurts my eyes to look at such gilded, sumptuous reflection. And yet everything has changed, and grandpa was right.

Your pa… All it takes is the pretty face of a fall morning for me to get all ginned up to dancing the deadly cogitating two-step—philosophizing and sentimentalizing—instead of doing the job I was supposed to do, talking to you both about the seasons. Time to get back to the task at hand.

Your old man looks at seasons as time-presents wrapped in the most magnificent bows imaginable. Open them with gusto and enjoy them as long as they're here. You know what a stickler your pa is about living now instead of racking up a whole slew of life IOU's that you half-heartedly mean to pay off later. Well, later is now. And it's a true rich man who understands that time is the only true coin of life's realm. So get out and open up these gift-seasons knowing your pa is around somewhere watching you both enjoy the grand unwrapping.

You've both got more than a fair idea of my kinship with autumn so…

Whenever the first days of fall appear (like this morning), please take your spouse or your kids, your best friend or your girlfriend, or boyfriend for that matter, and walk together through the driftleaves of autumn. Enjoy yourselves. Do something you haven't done before, or go someplace you haven't been. Saddle up the horses and take them to a part of the ranch you seldom visit, like Taku Flats or Ruster Ridge. If you haven't been there in years, drive up to the mountains to Lake Solitude or Hailey's Meadow. Have a nice dinner in town, maybe at McGraws or Colter's Chophouse. Remember: McGraws for the ribs and Colter's for the steaks. In any event, toast your old man and his love for the first days (and all the days) of autumn.

Thanksgiving—fall's finale. Best damn holiday of the year in my worldly estimation. Better than Christmas (you won't agree with me here until you're a heck of a lot older). Don't get me wrong. I really love Christmas. But to me Thanksgiving is the takes-the-cake top of the cat's meow. Of course, riding out to find the right Christmas tree with your mom is still unbeatable.

Thanksgiving is the sweet dickens because you get to eat the most heaven-sent homemade food ever made on mortal earth by the grace and love of your mom and grandma. Even angels have been known to have fisticuffs over your grandma's carrot cake—and her German turkey dressing. And I remember your mom, with all her Pennsylvania Dutch ancestors spiriting around the flour bowl as she churns out egg noodles and fresh baked biscuits that would tempt mister jack devil himself to sell his soul for an hour just to partake of your ma's fixings.

And the last pickings of the Winesaps and Spitzenburgs that my cousins gathered from the orchard, having been peeled, cut-up, nestled in their pie plates, now bake away in the pantry oven, perfuming the air with apple-pie essence and, mingling with the aromas of roast turkey, sweet potato pie, and green beans and bacon—one can almost eat the gorgeous flavors drifting out from the kitchen, and in every room throughout the house the air is suffused with the smell of Thanksgiving dinner. Just the memory alone makes your pa hungry.

With Thanksgiving you get to see members of the family tree you haven't seen in half of forever and talk to them in the old-fashioned way, face-to-face. Then, with every eye on the clock, Pa turns on the old Grundig and you listen to Nebraska score its first touchdown in the first minute and you know it's going to be another shutout. Then you toss together a pre-dinner hoops game on the dirt-baked basketball court behind the barn and find out whose grown old and who hasn't. Soon after, the youngest cousin is granted the privilege of clanging the dinner bell and bringing everyone to table. And Grandpa says grace, which is always a good grace, and your Uncle Tom as usual tacks on, "Rub-a-dub-dub, let's eat the grub," which makes everyone laugh even though they hear it every year. Some things just don't change. Sooooo, after the last giggle, and before you chow down, please toast my ghost and pass the cranberries.

Thanksgiving got me so hungry I had to momentarily quit my reminiscing to partake of breakfast, and refill my mug with another pour from the endless coffee pot. I can still hear those elk going at it. What a beautiful morning to be alive, Little Ones. Time for another season...

Winter. I crave fall, Little Ones, but I long for winter. Winter is the Viking in me that loves the fierce snow storm that wails against my body but also longs for the coming back to the homefire, and the sumptuous feast, and the enduring family protected deep inside the house. Winter is my memory as I watch my pa, in the early dark and colder-than-blixens morning, warming the horse bits atop the kitchen potbelly as mom cooks up a mound of breakfast for pa and all the hands. Then, saddling up for the day's work and ride, he gently places the warmed metal in the horses' mouths, the steam that slowly crickles out making them look like joyful dragons. Winter makes me dream deeply and I sleep deeply, with windows open and heaps of blankets upon me—and my wife next to me.

In reality, Little Ones, there are two winters. One made for kids; the other for adults. The one made for adults is always too cold and always too long. The one made for kids is always perfect. A kid winter is an endless and wild snow carnival where all the rides are free. Where every surface imaginable is a possible ice rink, ski slope, or toboggan run. Where the first and only rule is that if your parents don't call you in, you don't go in. Where snowball fights would last for hours until your hands became near-blue ice claws and you couldn't stop even if you wanted to save your fingers or your life, and always we somehow found the strength to haul off one more iceball at our sibling enemies. Where even the routine walk to the bus was made magical, as we'd luxuriate in the cold morning heat of a bright and sunny winter's day, fascinated by the ever endless tonal variations of the pinchy crunch-squeaks of our boots on the dry powder snow.

Skiing, now that's my kid winter, Little Ones. Especially zipping down Sooty's ridge like fast gone madly on those old wooden Norwegian plowbenders, the ones Uncle Jack brought back with him from the old country. Winter wasn't officially winter until the skis were prepped and made ready for go. Like feverish snow elves, all of us boys gladly hunkered down in the workshop, the air permeated with the sapburnt crackle-smell of pine tar being scorched onto hickory and lignestone undersides, the lava-like black pitch bubbling on the wood, stirring the glee of all boys who idolized volcanoes and ached to fly down hills as fast as falcons, and the smell filled our nostrils with perfect kid memory.

The tippy tippy tippy-top of kid winter is, of course, Christmas. (Christmas, like winter, is divided accordingly. Kids know there is before-Christmas and Christmas itself. After-Christmas is strictly for adults, because that's when their winter begins.) Christmas— by any true kid definition (and your pa's memory)— started with absolutely no school. Christmas was, with Pa, the ritual putting up of all those almost edible, candy-colored Christmas lights, both outside and inside the house (and even in the barn for the horses and momma cow). Your pa loved the glow of those lights so much that I had my own special strand of blue glows just to stick up in my bedroom. Christmas was all us of boys helping ma decorate the bell, reindeer, tree, and little church Christmas cookies with red, blue, green, and white sugar frosting and then sprinkling them with those little sugar silver balls that looked like bb's and sounded great cracking against our teeth, for the truth is when you're a kid, noise always makes food taste better. Christmas eve was cooked goose and cabbage. Aunt Lynnette would play Bing Crosby and his White Christmas on the upright, and Grandma (and eventually the rest of us) would listen to the Mormon Tabernacle Choir on KSL out of Salt Lake City (for which Grandpa would invariably intone, "that station's been there since heck was a pup," and to which I had no idea who or what heck was). Of course, Christmas was never kid-complete without the anticipation and fixation of present-getting, and the Christmas eve sacrament of putting out snickerdoodles, a glass of milk, and a little side-snort of Jack Daniel's best to somehow induce Santa Claus to stay long enough for us to get a glimpse of him and maybe his reindeer.

And Christmas was ultimately, and will always be, the grand Christmas tree hunt. Saddling the horses on a bright blue, god-blessed day in the thrall of miles of white-feather powder snow. Fixing up the pbj's and wrapping them up in wax paper, then filling the thermoses with hot cocoa for us boys and coffee for the adults. Papa always said that the perfect Christmas tree was just aching to find us, and somehow it always did. We'd light out for the beautiful Diane lakes in early morning, and then cross over Cutter's pass by afternoon. And there, just a mile or so down slope, seemed to grow a heaven's crop of the best Christmas pines in the whole wide world. And somehow and always and soon thereafter, the perfect tree did appear. As per ritual, each of us boys got in two chops, pa as many as were needed, and then mom would finish it off with the champagne chop, and the tree would fall with a satisfying whoosh and whomp onto the powdery snow. A cinch of the rope around the trunk, a dally around the horn, and soon the lot of us were riding home with the perfect tree dragging behind us and the perfect Christmas still awaiting us.

Now I jump like a madman to summer because why not dream of summer in the middle of winter.

The grand hoo-hah of summer is the Fourth of July where it's time to break out a good cigar and make yourself a Gibson. If anyone gives you grief about the stogie, tell them you're smoking a cigar for your old man and to go eat a monkey-prune pie. And damn the teetotalers and bless the whiskey-makers for I'm going to tell you how to make the drink of drinks. A Gibson is a little piece of manna here on earth when it's made properly.

My old friend Jim knows exactly how. It's a dying art and he's one of the last craftsmen. Track him down if you need help. He checks in every other solstice and the occasional leap year. He weaned me on this extract of bob-wire in another epoch. In the time of pterodactyls and Elvis Presley. Vodka—a whisper of dry vermouth—straight up and naked as the day. Three onions. Not two. Not four. Three. Let's keep the saints happy. And dry, dry, dry. A drink as pretty as a picture postcard—all New York'ed and Paris'ed—and drinking it should be just as wonderful as staring at it.

Now dream up a damn fine toast about life, love, liberty and the pursuit of happiness, and some added extravagance about how much I loved life and that if I were there right now what I would be doing, which I'm sure will elicit any amount of commentary from your uncles, and that would be just about normal. You figure it out. I like the Fourth because I enjoy seeing a slew of fireworks starbursting over my head. And your Uncle Tom, the pyro man, putting on his fiery show just for the doing. Ask your grandma and grandpa to regale you with some of Uncle Tom's firework escapades. Or ask your Uncle Mike or Uncle Adam. If I could watch Uncle Tom's fireworks again, I'm sure I could make it back to earth for a couple hour's visit.

And how could I forget about spring. Spring is a time to make up a big bouquet of flowers for someone you love, or are trying to love, or are in love with. Give them with a jigger of surprise and a grin and a kiss, and you'll earn the glow of flowers upon her face. Begin the giving on the first day of spring. Since you're my son, you'll never lose by a bouquet given. Ask your mom and she'll tell you what the spring solstice means to her. And since you're my daughter, go surprise some guy and bring him flowers. It's good to turn a man on his head every now and then. Keeps him guessing. Keeps him awake. You don't have to toast me this time. Just go celebrate spring, and your old man will smile the smile of the heavens.

The grand toasting and starbursting fireworks, the dry Gibsons and endless flower giving, the egg noodles and sweet German turkey and Nebraska football, the glowly Christmas lights and the daring fast skis and the always waiting for Santa—these are our seasons—these habits of celebration so needed to remind us that we are alive, and that it's good to be alive. And this being alive, it's something I've more than once forgotten to do, and am only now remembering to do again. It's never too late to begin, my Little Ones. Never.

I love you both.

—Pa

September 3

5:48 a.m.
38 degrees

A Most Important Letter

Dear Little Ones,

SUNRISE — A TIME when all truths are still clean and enviable. Thankful that I have coffee and cabin to sustain me, and pen and paper to write another letter. Just plain thankful.

A time will come in your life when you know you must reveal, confess, or lay open your innermost thoughts and feelings to another person. It may be to admit a long and simmering crush or love. Or to atone for some lie or act of disloyalty. Or it may be to damn someone who has hurt you deeply or betrayed you.

You dream incessantly of the perfect moment and place and configuration of planets to begin the revelation. You constantly mumble to yourself variations of what you'd like to say, which you expurgate, re-edit, and then re-mumble to yourself. You endlessly cajole, curse, berate, beguile, and manipulate yourself to no end. You drink yourself courageous. You flounder in imagined rejections. Your gut becomes twisted. Your heart bangs for attention. And your soul wanders like a Dickens ghost looking for a way back home.

You need to speak your piece. But you fear your mouth. You fear the mutiny of your tongue, teeth, lungs, brain, and adrenal gland that will force you to utter words that you did not dream of, rewrite, or plan for. And even if you could quell this mutiny and your words came flying out of your mouth in perfect condition, well then—

—Upon hitting air, these words are likely to undergo strange auditory and emotional permutations on their long trip up into your listener's head, where they will remain brazenly modified or mysteriously altered beyond all recognition.

What you need to say does not require the immediate consideration of, or diplomacy from, the other person. You do not crave his or her arguments or tears. Or interruptions or excitations. Or even an answer. You just need them to stop and listen to you—to make them think. But nothing, except perhaps a gun to the head, will stop them dead in their tracks faster than your words put down on paper. What you then need so desperately to say doesn't dare be said. It needs to be written.

And good or bad, your letter will always be read because people are human, and we can't seem to turn our head away from an accident coming, or turn down the possibility of a straight flush on the next deal. We take to a letter like a dog to a bone. Anxious to find some faraway and secretive corner to sit down and begin the gnaw.

This letter you must write—

This letter is you made paper and ink.

This letter carries weight. Unlike mouth-words which are made of air and have no place to go but into the ether.

This letter holds time. Your God-given time. The minutes and hours you took to craft and weigh your words, to create sentences true, clear, and powerful. Your time has gone onto the paper and into the ink, and that is what the person will have of you. You as time.

This letter is not easy. But being brave is not supposed to be easy. It is godawful fierce work to explore your jungle of thoughts and emotions, to work your way through the tangle of your half lies and partial truths, to eventually track down your most honest thoughts, capture them intact, and finally bring them to paper.

This letter is real. The person who receives it can actually hold—in his or her hands—you and your thoughts. Can re-read it, re-touch it, re-crumble it, or re-pocket it. Or even toss, tear, or burn it—but they'll certainly have to read it.

This letter you must write by hand. For when you

"write," your words come directly from your body, head, and heart, which all combine to put your humanity on the page. You are the mistakes that are halfway scratched out. You are the Romanesque capitals made at the beginning of each sentence. You are the words that stay perfectly on the line, or the sentence that slants either up or down. You are the doodles made in the margins, or the coffee stain on the last paragraph. All of these are who you are. The visible anguish and excitement of this letter you must write.

And when you have expunged and exhausted your passions, or lamentations, or damnations, then you are done. Let your words take a vacation. Let them sit in the sun for a couple of days—get a tan—relax. Maybe even let them have a week off.

When you are good and ready, read yourself—who you are and what you have said. Let the cool of your reason now scrutinize your ink-forged emotions and thoughts. And when you find peace in all of your words, then that is the right time to send off your letter—or to not send it at all. For sometimes, strangely enough, this letter you need to write is ultimately a letter you need only "send" to yourself—for yourself. And through all the headwork, hard work, and heartbreak of trying to write this letter for some-one else, you ultimately decide that the person who truly needed to hear you the most was you. Only you can know how much peace you will bring to yourself by sending or not sending this letter of yours.

Yet whatever happens afterwards, you will always know the courage of having joined the conviction of your thoughts to the perseverance of your pen. When you ventured to be honest to yourself. And in the end you cannot ask more of yourself than the truth told and the truth revealed. And that is why you must write this letter.

And that is why I write these letters to you.

Papa

Y OUR VOICE — INSIDE my head but a moment ago, and now you must be off to dreamland. So sleepy. Your body… Warm and glowing. Under cool white sheets. All of you lying there before me, now here—as vividly as if you were beside me…

I remember…

Where were you in that long ago? As I waited there, all young buck in a warm summer night, atop the big hill where we learned to kiss. The car hood still coal-warm under my legs. Where were you as I lay pitched back against the tinted-blue and highway-cold window. With the click, click, click of a cooling 428 metal universe underneath me.

A burgeoning crescent moon squinting, and the chirpy patriotic refrains of Sousa music echoing from hand-held Panasonics made in Japan and from the tinny car stereo ensconced in the belly of my night-sleek and languid Bonneville. Ragtop, of course. Crisp, cold beer stings my tongue as I utter a silent toast to you under the spilling fireworks of Meteor Stars, Platinum Spiderwebs, cannonade-blue to inken-red Double-Petal Peonies and Silver Pearl Serpents flying through the celestial biology of colossal, exploding, green-red-purple

Chrysanthemums. My mind wanders to this same night of last summer. To the savory image of fireworks glowing upon your skin, shoulders naked and glistening. What is it about these fireworks.

I remember—

A rowboat in the middle of a lake on that Fourth of July. Murmuring anticipations from unseen gatherings upon the shore. A midsummer's night with the lapping of the waves against the gunnels. Resting idly. Not really moving. Looking up at the stars (and there are so many stars to see). Cradled by the boat. You leaning back with your head next to mine. My arms around you. Your hot summer skin upon my chest. Cool air from the black/blue water. Slowly I take your hand so cool and small within mine. Fingers twine and dip into the water. Crack— crack—and boom—the fireworks erupt. The sky shatters in color. The stars now electric. And I wish we could row straight up into those wild explosions and color and elec- tricity and pirouette within them and around them for a small eternity.

Big grinny five-year-old smiles on our faces. The sky-world Krazy-Kat like a Verdi grand opera but made just for madly mad children who would jump on stage in emerald lederhosen, pop red balloons with cinna- mon toothpicks, and gribbly sing in verhooten verse. Boys, just keep those fireworks going. All night if you have to, or if you want to. Just keep them magiferical and giddybluebowschuss, as if all the universe could be this much fun. The water shimmers with all the toothsome, tasty, red, gold, and green that pour from the sky. Hell, the show looks as good on the lake as it does in the heavens.

The finale arrives. Always too early. Never long enough. But it is all and everything we wanted. An incredible catastrophe of magnificence and jewelry. You almost want to bawl for delight because it's all so resplendent and incandescent, spanglorious and grandacious, and all sorts of other diamond and ruby words. You figure if there is a god, he'd better have fireworks like this in heaven, or you'll turn your wings back in. And the boom and the smoke. Jumping right through your bones. Like all craziness and war and delirium and love, and heaven knows what else, but at this moment you really don't give a damn because your eyes are oooooooing and ahhhhing just like the rest of your body. Like the biggest damn climax you could ever imagine, and you're sitting right pretty in the middle of it all, gasping like the rest of the thousands who are Yankee Doodle Dandying right along with you. One big hooting, screaming metropolis caught in the momentum of a cataclysmical, Kingdom-Comery conflagration.

And then, like the P. T. Barnamous and Ringlingary Boys that those firework lads truly are, they take your Grimm Brothers and Mother Gooses down the pyro path of hoodwinkery to where you most certainly believe that the big show must really be over. You sense the collective pause and a thousand-thousand, wiggling, giggling stomachs. Everyone wanting one more lickety-split and blue-ribbon special. And then those merry-makers let loose every volcano left at their disposal, illuminating each and every twinkly, sparkly, Santa Claus face staring skyward. You are those red-letter fountains of flame, and the goose-quilled darts of gold, and the sparking champagne fizzi-gigs. And you are the boom—and the capping powder—and the quivering prism lake—and the child gasp—and the U.S. of A—and every thing and everything else. And the world continues to roar even after the last streaks of light rip across your eyes, leaving optical sparklers in your head. Now that's a finale. That's living, baby. A flag-waving, God-bless-America, pyrotechnicalacious banquet of goodness-gracious and Jiminy Christmas, and more apple-pie kisses, beer-breath hugs, and innocent memories than any poor slob of a human ever deserves. Amen.

The clock has turned a minute from before. Where are you now? Deep in the midst of some dream parade of fireworks and rowboat and water-dipped hands? Splash and boom and color and smoke? There's a dream worth dreaming. And these words are like the visible embers from my stove fire crackling into the night and stars. With God and soul and the rapture of it all igniting the

red-arrow bull's-eye of your beauty, heart, and memory. A
big smile on your face. And your eyes with all the colors
of the galaxies blazing and burning within all that's left of
my galaxy dreaming.

Night

Little Ones,

I FOUND THIS POEM among my notes. I wrote it for your mother a long time ago. I can't seem to make out the title. It looks as if a certain mouse had himself a refined dinner plan—because the only words he left unnibbled were desert and rain. And that is where it was written. In the desert, in the rain, where your mother and I rode together long ago.

Riding under blue-burnt rain
falling on umber back and mane
heaven pour your manna sweet
upon our tongues and naked feet.

Fill the body, baptismal rain
in sheeted fury enfold our flame
your tacit wind in angel consent
bears desert spice from earthen wet.

Rose-blue this sky, shepherd rain—
your east and west now rainbow-tamed
now gallows dusk turns monochrome
and signals both heart and soul to home.

—Papa

WIND SWEEPING NOW over my bare back. My feet wet as I tread upon the music-grass, so cool and dew-laden. I can almost see the valley's solitude. And my pen faithfully confiding these sensations to night paper. So much quiet, everywhere, I feel that I am drinking it into me like some chalice-wine.

An autumn apple moon, quarter-bitten, lies lopsided in the night's turning. And how do I describe clouds that look like a sound? Like a Chopin nocturne glissading in ghost-dance notes across the pale courtyard of charcoal-dust heavens. I can't believe how magnificent it feels to be this alive. That God allows me to feel so much of his earth and sky.

How dangerous it is to be so aware. When the greatest strength imaginable is being able to feel this deeply. And, for the first time, you are given the pain of being completely awake. Knowing you can never return to your slumber—ever. That one has slept in one's body for ever so long, waiting to wake up and never knowing how or if one will. Like possessing diamonds that you can't see unless you wear diamond glasses. And now I am fully awake. And alive. And everywhere, diamonds.

I wish I could wrap up the glitter star-green of this moment and hand it to you like an angel gift. Give you the heat lightning flying in jagged silence over the distant mountains. And the smell of September prairie grass and the even fainter scent of October pine now descending. And the whir and purr of the windmill blades in the distant blackness. Give you the invisible sage wind whisking past your cheeks. And the cricket quartets and frog symphonies that play near the creek's edge. To collect these sensations like a scientist of the soul and give them to you in their finest hour of coincidence and destiny.

I wish I could give this night to you. The truth of being so alive. But then I wish I could have many wishes. I wish I could keep walking far into God's night, and never stop. And I wish I could continue to live forever. And I wish, the biggest wish of all, that I could be with you right now.

September 8
7:19 a.m.
raining

There Are Hard Days to Live

Dear Little Ones,

I WOKE UP THIS MORNING not feeling much like living. The fire's gone out, it's raining outside, and I'm feeling a bit poorly. I wouldn't want you to see me like this. But then again, this is who I am—at this moment in my life—and I want you to know your pa for all of who he is. Living isn't always red bows and birthday balloons. Sometimes it's just plain hard. And this is also part of what you should know. About how difficult, wearisome, and fearful life can be. I love you both.

There are hard days to live.

You awake to a day when you feel you've done it all before, and you're going to do it again, so why do it at all.

You might wake up a little sick, but not much.

Money might be a little tighter than usual.

Your heart might be a little more lonely.

Maybe things aren't going as well as they could be, or you've been hit with a spate of small disagreeables. Maybe life is okay in general, but still a minor conspiracy of ill fortune seems to have been visited upon your head.

Or it just might be that deep in that belly of yours, you know that something isn't quite right, that you can't quite figure "it" out, and that you're not quite sure what "it" is. And you know you can't solve the problems of the world, or your world, or any world that morning, so you lie there, eyes open, alarm ringing, staring into the darkness, wondering where to begin as the sun and stars hang momentarily in primordial balance.

There are hard days to live.

When moving from the comfort of your warm cocoon bed into a cold and steel world seems like the most gargantuan effort in the universe, and you wonder where Superman went to and why he can't jerk you up out of your malaise, or why miracles don't seem to fall into your lap as they used to or seemed to, and you question whether you can really start this day or not.

When work looms up ahead of you like a jail sentence. Or when school seems like a preparation for the chain gang. For age gives no free limousine rides here.

Then there are people you must talk to, meet with, and move among, when you must go out into the world to make your living by cooperating with humanity, and just that thought alone makes you want to curl up into the smallest possible ball of yourself, tuck the covers back underneath you, and become so invisible that you feel you don't really exist and that everyone has forgotten you—and you are convinced that the day never really began or possibly was never even created.

Still you get up and begin to move, for we must all dance the same dance. And we make it through—somehow. As we always do.

There are hard days to live.

Sometimes your body is just plain tired.

It might be the tired of laboring like a harnessed ox at the grist mill, forced to go around in endless circles just to move the mill wheel and grind the flour.

It might be the tired of being stretched too thin. When there's only one of you, and you need ten of you, and even that might not be enough. Where everything is being measured in increments of you, and you seem to be slicing yourself up into finer and finer pieces until you've become nothing but microscopic mash.

It might be the tired of not enough sleep. When your world demands that you work a forty-eight hour day and you were only made for twenty-four. When the thought of sleep fills you with more apprehension than anticipation because you haven't crossed your last "t", dotted your last "i" or curled your last "q" — When you act like you're immortal when in fact you're only mortal.

It might be the tired of living so long. As when you get older and know too much, and are closer to the end then you are to the beginning. As when you feel that your body's main duty is to carry what's left of your mind around like some precious orb.

It might be the tired of the old ways but the not quite certain about how to get to the new ways. About how to track down the rumors of possible happiness and satisfaction. Of where to find the precious morsel of nirvana known as living. You know there's got to be a better way of life—somewhere, sometime, somehow—but you're not exactly sure what better is.

You might want more time in your life to attempt the things you like to do, and not just perform the things you have to do. You might want more money to smooth out the edgy corners of your financial existence. Or you might want to explore your thoughts and ideas and heart with another person and see what that constellation is all about.

Time.

Money.

Love.

All these needs. And we know we must satisfy them.

There are hard days to live.

When you're losing or have lost someone you care

for or love.

When you're terribly sick and there's no one to take care of you.

When you're badly injured and you'd prefer to order a new body, if there was one available.

When your heart is breaking all over the damn place, and then finally is broken. When starting over again in life seems like asking for angelic dispensation, and you know all the angels are on strike.

And Superman doesn't come to the rescue, and the old miracles don't happen anymore, and no angels emerge to sit on your shoulder.

When being alive seems like a cruel choice, and sometimes an hour is the limit of your existence, and sometimes even a minute is just too much. When ultimately you're just left with yourself and the moment, and that's the grand total of what you seem to own in the world.

It's just that sometimes living seems too damn hard. And you wonder how to keep on doing it.
Day after day after day.

There are hard days to live.
And sometimes they will be just a few, and sometimes they will seem endless.
And eventually you'll come to understand that

we've all been here before—or more than likely are going there now. And maybe that idea will make it easier for you, and maybe it won't. But there will still be hard days to live, and you will still have to find your way through them.

You start by trying, minute by minute, if that's all you can do.

And if you fail, you start again.

For this is a fight within yourself and for yourself.

And to fight for something means to fall and pick yourself up again and again.

We may not always fight well, and some days we may not be able to fight at all, but somehow we find out what we are made of by trying and beginning again.

And then move on. Through any and all of these hard days.

In one way or another.
Somehow.
To somewhere.
Someway.

September 15
4:49 a.m.
29 degrees

My Littlest Ones,

I WANT TO HAVE SO MANY memories of you. To imagine being your father and not some cabin-bound hermit who at the end of his days realizes the immensity of his regrets-to-be.

Let my memories of you be like water on the moon. A beautiful impossibility— but allowing me to sleep and dream of infinite beginnings rather than Othello endings.

Thus, I want to remember…

How I tucked you into bed at night. Then acted out the pages from some old dime-store Western that I had lying about. Made the bad parts not so bad and the good guys really good. Strummed out some new western warble on the git-fiddle for you, maybe two if the mood really hit me. But as usual I got in trouble with your mom for keeping you up past your bedtime, and had to sheepishly promise to quit for the night.

I want to remember the bright blue-sky winter days when the sun was hot on our backs and the air felt like ice cubes upon our faces. When for fun, we'd tie a goldline rope to the back of the pickup, click you kids into your skis, and tow you on the snow-packed roads leading out to the feeding grounds. Just like your grandpa did for me when I was a boy, except he used Cayenne, who grew wise in the ways of being able to somehow jerk the line and make us kids do faceplows rather than snowplows.

Teaching you both in front of the mirror at the ripe age of two how to make baby bobcat and Brahmer bull faces just as Aunt Melody once showed us kids. (Which for some odd reason was an endless source of entertainment for your pa even at the worldly age of eleven.)

Smelling your newness upon this earth. The baby-Jesus smell as Grandma used to put it. Pure. Unsullied. Like the imagined smell in the twirling air of eiderdown feathers spin-floating around the yard on a new spring day.

I want to remember warming your two a.m. bottle, clipping your locks, watching you be baptized, bathing you in the big porcelain sink... how I often laid you against my chest and felt the cradlesong of your tiny breaths as you fell asleep.

How I watched your new-found locomotion of tumble-and-trip steps—when down you would fall over and over again, crying until you realized that no one was going to come to your rescue, and thus you had to pick yourself up on your own. Both of us learning that a part of love is letting you fall —over and over again.

I want to remember your pre-sleep galavantings in your Roy Roger and Trigger PJ's which, having been wind-dried, were permeated with the autumn smells of whitebark pine, ox-eye daisies, and yellow sweet clover. After hearing you recite your prayers of heavenly insurance to take you through the night unscathed, I would attempt to serenade you to sleep. And satisfied that my show had been a sleeping success, I would then hear lone voices springing forth from the darkness, recalling me to the stage for an encore.

The excitement of teaching you how to whistle "Oh Susanna," or coo like a mourning dove, or read a compass and a map so you'd never get lost in the mountains, or measure the rain in the rain gauge out by the barn and then mark it down. Teaching you how to ride a bike, drive the truck in haying season, or recite Robert Frost poems—but not necessarily in that order.

How I cut your hair to a summer stubble on the front porch just like my pappy did to me, remembering how strange the hum and zizzle of the electric bees had sounded then, seemingly hidden somewhere inside the sheep shears. How I rubbed my best Kentucky bourbon on your hurting gums while you were teething. Showed you where the old man in the moon lives and explained how he got there. Brought home little road gifts when I was working out-of-state, receiving your blackmail kisses of love while you wondered what I'd brought you.

Overhearing you chirp to your mom like sparrows about the goings-on at the schoolhouse, or your ribbon-to-be state fair yearlings, or your newest trials and tribulations in the world of ten-year-old romance.

I want to remember how I was there at the exact moment when, with startled oooohhs and wows, you jaw-dropped and wide-eyed-gasped at your first falling star. And how I tried to align your little eyeballs up and past my pointer finger to spy your first satellite beelining it across the night sky. Later your mom and I, sitting side by side on the birch bench next to the fishpond, cradled our two temporarily exhausted sources of pure energy while we all watched showers of meteors crazing through the endless summer darkness.

This is what I wish I could remember, my Little Ones.

M AY I TELL YOU something? I'm amazed that I sit here under this third full moon, realizing that I'm still alive. I can't be sure of how many moons I have left. I can't truly imagine that this is the last one. I'm still not ready to leave this earth.

Look at the autumn moonlight on the aspens. My god, it seems like Christmas. I've never seen such beauty, and I want to share it with you. Such a mercury-silver shining upon these September leaves. Pretty as a Christmas tree. With grin-twinkly, shiny sparks. Hundreds and thousands of twirling lights all across the valley and up onto the ridges. And the imps and elves seem to be choreographing the puppetry of each leaf's twist, yaw, and twinkle in the gusts of warm breeze. I'm awe-struck that the hand of Providence would create such a floorshow for the mere reason of beauty. I feel damn-fool lucky to be amidst such sparkle. I want to remain here as long as possible. To entertain even the mere hope of redemption—which is what we all long for, and we never know how much we want it until it's not ours to have.

Now I feel a sudden Muir wind coming off some king-blue icecap and glacier dance, swept down from vast summits. I smell granite, spicy wet, gathered from the walls of distant canyons, tempered by the fall ponderosa pine still sweetly baked from summer. The wind drapes over me in emperor silk, and never before have I smelled such a manna made on earth.

Walk with me now into this very bright night, and revere with me in silence what must be God-given and what is surely God-taken.

My Love,

Will you remember?

Past, Present, that must fade
toward valleys that will give ...
the house during ...
... might ...
When glance on ... yet ago
... concerns,
as ... we go,
ever ... looking back.

Winter. . .

October 2
5:32 a.m.

Starting the Day

Good Morning, Little Ones,

I WOKE UP THIS MORNING to the door wide open. I must not have closed it all the way last night. Lucky me. Because I'm watching from my bed a most amazing theater—the falling of the biggest, fattest, slowest, snowflakes I have ever seen. Lazily lazy, like feather elephants, elegantly dawdling on their way to work.

Autumn—from rainstorms, to sunshine, to snowfalls and back again. Why do you think your old man loves this season so much? Look at this layer of frost on my blanket, and thick enough to scrape ice doodles on it. I sure hope the coals in the stove are still hot. Then again, what's the hurry. There is none and that's the point. The bed is warm and I'm not dead. Not a bad way to start the day. I think I should praise all the house sprites who conspired to open the front door, delivering me to this most exquisite spectacle. Thank God for being alive this morning.

Starting the day—
Another chance to be new again.
How many of us still wish for that?
To be your own sunrise.
To awaken like a prayer—both solemn and joyful at
still being alive.

Pretending that Santa might have arrived in the
middle of the night and you couldn't wait to wake up just
before dawn—or even earlier.

Pretending that you're a puppy whose only reason to
exist is to wag its tail in perpetual doggy bliss, anticipat-
ing the next petting session.

Pretending that you're wildly dreaming of that most
perfect and gossamer moment of a first kiss.

Can you be this excited—again and again?
Can you start each day like this?
Why not?
Who says you can't?
What do you have to lose?

Sometimes we make being happy so difficult.
And being thankful such a chore.
Starting the day like a job we hate.
Beginning it like swallowing ten tablespoons of
devil-made cough syrup.
Because, somehow along the way, we forget that

being alive and healthy and happy are noble goals—or just good ideas.

And that the opposite of being alive is being dead.

What a choice.

So open the day like a Christmas present waiting. Or a puppy needing petting. Or a new kiss a-wanting.

Open the back door, step out onto the porch, and greedily suck in some new air from this new day. It's free and there's lots of it.

Start with a brand new good-morning. To your husband or your wife. To your kids. To those you work with—and don't work with.

What's the harm?

How difficult is it? And it isn't, and you know it. So do it.

And make it a habit.

As hokey as it may sound, you have it good—You just have to remember how good.

Another chance to live—
How damn lucky can you get.
So don't wait for someone to put a gun to your head, or a disease to your body.
Try the simple way.
Wake up. Be thankful.
For whatever happens on this day, you are endlessly

given the chance to start again—to be alive.
And all of us should wish for that.

Love,
Papa

10:00 a.m.
Starting to warm up.

On My Boy Becoming a Man

My Son,

As YOUR PAPA, I have so much to tell you, to show you, of what it means to become a man. Trying to answer all your curious-boy questions about the day's mysteries and wonders with the perfect papa-given mix of accuracy, simplicity, and clarity. Watching you fall and stand and then fall again as all boys must do with such ferocity and perpetuity, to occasionally pick you up but not too often. Leading you through the long fire that is baptism of my son becoming a man. And somehow I must do all of this through the mortality of my words.

By your mom's grace and nearness, your sister will learn her mother wisdom. In one way or another, my Son, I must find a way to be next to you. Flying across a massive canyon of memory and time, hoping with all the strength, clarity, and love I can forgather as your father, I hope these words will wisely guide you toward someday becoming your own man.

Somehow, my Son, in our breakneck lust for the future of now, we got it into our heads that, like pushing a button or dialing a number, becoming a man is easy. Just devour a few dozen man-becomes-hero movies, pick-up a fast-looking car, make out with a girl or girls, pocket a few bucks, and do whatever you want whenever you want—easy. As a consequence, we turn out the perfect someone who looks like a man, talks like a man, and even sounds like a man but somehow acts like a Jack Sprat Billy-boy stunted at the pinnacle of his manly maturation, some-where between the hormonal apex of twelve to twenty-three, who has no want, inclination, or motivation to earn his stripes and become a full-fledged, grown-up, thinking, thoughtful, good man. Now I'm not saying you have to be the Pope's boy scout or John Wayne's muleskinner, but if you're not learning or wanting to someday become a man, then you're forever practicing to remain a boy.

Even the very notion of becoming a man can seem quaint and old-fashioned, lying somewhere between the dusty dignity of fairytale honor practiced by creaky and ancient medieval knights, and the somewhat myth-made glory and born-in-the-blood courage of a cowboy's rawhide toughness and his ever infallible code of right and wrong. So all this man-becoming might get to seem a little too over-the-top, far-fetched, movie-made, and history-old. You might begin to wonder what's so all-fired important about becoming a man, when, you'll be one anyhow and someday soon. Because, my son, it's not being a man that makes a man, it's the becoming. And this becoming can only be given as a series of tests. And someone must decide and believe you are ready enough to take these tests. And you must decide and believe you can pass these tests. My first real test began shortly after my fourteenth year of existence—my last summer to be a boy.

I remember that summer had peculiarity to it. Like shaking a snow globe except you shook only falling sunbeams, and you knew you'd never see that again. I remember how much I loved being back here at the cabin with grandpa, once again working the summer high pasture, yet feeling like I was growing a foot a day, and not my usual one inch a year. Grandpa allowed me to ride fence alone, doctor the calves as I saw fit, and even once saddle his mare, Cayenne, (which I had never, ever done before). He also suffered me to cook almost every dinner and breakfast, make a stagger at the day's coffee (which he also had me constantly taste so I'd know what black dirt and horseshoe was supposed to taste like), and had me put up more firewood than I could ever remember. I even became a real doctor, when during a tangled ruckus between a fence and yearling, Grandpa got the south end of a deep gash and I had to sew him up. He dropped that needle and thread into my hand like it was day-old bread change, suggesting that I make the stitches tight. What a strange feeling to have your grandpa's life in your hands, or what felt like his life. After that stitching and all that summer, I felt more a man and grown-up than ever.

But what I didn't know was that I was the main carpenter in the house of my own making—a blueprint conjured up long ago between my pa and grandpa. And that these newly-granted responsibilities and supposed freedoms I thought I so justly deserved were only part of the grand covenant, obligation, and pact between fathers and sons, grandpas and grandsons, and between all men and all boys wanting to become men. The responsibilities given are the tests all boys must pass to earn the trust of all men. And these tests had started the day I was born, and were as old as man itself.

A few days after my fated fourteenth birthday and while rebuilding a gate near the corrals, grandpa informed me he was heading to town. He didn't say we—and I heard that loud enough. Bam!—like a time-trick machine, I was suddenly standing on a giant cliff overlooking my entire future—and the bottom was all fog and clouds. When your hero, guardian, and living legend (to my own thinking)—the man who could help birth baby calves in a fall blizzard, fend off a grouchy black bear with his bowie knife (another letter and story I hope), and teach you about Mozart, Mars, and making split-rail apple pie—hands you the keys to the kingdom, you don't say no. You can't look like you're some bottomless-pit-falling, henhearted, spitless, stone-white shaking idiot of a boy. You can't and I couldn't because here I was being offered and beholden to the only thing any boy ever truly wants—without sometimes really knowing how much he truly wants it—the trust to becoming one's own man. But boy, did this boy know it.

Just before grandpa rode off, and with his Sermon-on-the-Mount stare, he delivered his instructions.

"Think. Like your pa. Not like an ax. Or a hammer. If you get into trouble, think. If you don't get in trouble, think. Stupid will hurt you. Smart will save you. And it's your job now to be smart. I trust you, Boy." And that was that, and I remember what he said about trust and thinking and trouble like it was the Lord's Prayer rubbed permanent into my brain.

So what did I do? I thought. About everything, even sleeping and breathing. And I was smart. Smarter than I thought I ever could be. And I avoided trouble like a boy avoids broccoli and girls. Was I scared? You bet your roses I was. And did I do my job? Without a hitch, as if I were grandpa and pa all rolled into one. And my reward after five days? The best reward of all—a grandpa grin, a grandpa commentary ("looks like no one died"), a big pat on the back, and a "your pa would be proud of you." That was a full house of compliments in my book, and I took every last one of them to my now grown-man's heart. I knew I had passed the test. But what your papa didn't know was how many tests there were still to pass to become a man, and that somehow these tests never truly end.

So when do you become a man, my Son?

Do you become a man by running around buck-naked in the wilderness for a week, waiting for some god-vision of three crows riding bareback on a bull elk at sun's rising? Do you become a man by going to war to bludgeon, shoot, bayonet, or shish-kabob some dumb kid your own age on the other side who also thought going to war would make him a man? Do you become a man by souping up the latest Chevy with a 327 under the hood and whipping some poor sod in a midnight street drag?

No, you become a man when you first decide to put away the things of childhood, the talk of childhood, and the thoughts of childhood. You decide because you cannot be treated as both a man and a boy. Because you are either one or the other, but you are not both. And it doesn't matter your age—you can be a child at fifteen or forty. Only when you as a boy decide you're done waiting for the man you want to be and start being the man you want to become, do you begin to become a man.

When do you become a man?
When you become your own man.
When other men trust you to do a man's work. Trust

you with their name, their reputation, their thoughts. Trust you to watch their backs and trust you with their lives.

To become a man is to carry out your word because you gave your word. And your word is you as a man.

You become a man the moment you understand that responsibility is a real and vital commitment to yourself and others, and not some lazy-dog, all-agreeing grunt.

Becoming a man means doing the right thing even though it may be hard or difficult. Boys do what is easiest. A man does what is right, whether easy or not.

When do you become a man?

You become a man when you marry not just for love but to be a partner with your wife. To be the best man you can be with her, and when you fall short, to admit your shortcomings and to constantly strive to be a great man to your wife.

You become a man when, in having children, you not only physically look after and protect them but also protect them with all the love and learning you have to give.

You become a man when you give your family the best of who you are. And ultimately by being the best man to yourself and to your wife, you are being the best man to your children. And that, my Son, is a great gift and responsibility.

And what type of man should you be, my Son?

A good man. Above all else, strive to be a good man.

And you do not become a good man overnight.

Much like a big, solid Douglas fir you must learn to withstand all manner of wind, rain, lightening, sun, and even fire—year after year after year—and still stand tall and true.

A good man, in your papa's book, is a great man.

One who constantly strives to be the best of men, to himself and to others. Because the world can never have enough good men.

And what makes a good man, my Son.

A good man is being fair. In both your words and your actions.

When you admit being wrong. And then right that wrong.

A good man knows when he's been humbled, and learns from his humility.

Being a good man means to speak with sincerity, and love with certainty.

A good man will try to act wisely by thinking first and then acting.

A good man tells the truth.

A good man lives for the joy in life and the happiness of being alive, not shackled to the wants of the future or the regrets of the past.

A good man defends those that cannot defend themselves.

And a good man knows the difficulty of being a man, knowing the fall from grace is always near at hand, and thus is always striving to make himself a better man.

And as I quickly grow older, my Son, I see that the becoming a man and the being a man are eventually and truly one in the same, and the tests and the testing never end. I know in my father heart, and in all the other places I cannot go to at this moment, that I believe in you with all my love, even as time now disappears before me. And I know someday you will become a man to make your papa proud—your own man. Walking true to your own beliefs, carrying your name proudly, ever loyal to a valiant heart, and believing that being a good man in this life is a great endeavor. And on that day, I will somehow be with you. And somehow, I will have been your father. I love you.

Papa

Night
All calm and snow-beautiful.

Travel the World

Dear Little Ones,

I FEEL LIKE THIS PEN OF MINE is on fire this cold evening. Blazing though the night like a Christmas meteor... ready to take me anywhere and everywhere that I long to go. Remembering, as if it were but seconds ago, the exact moment my love of travelling began.

That crazy-luscious childhood memory... my folks driving late into some cold fall night while my brothers and I, like large mounds of sleeping dogs, were cocooned under a pile of blankets, sleeping bags, quilts, and bed-rolls in the back of the ice-aired station wagon, lullabied to sleep by the ever reliable metal drone of a made-in-Detroit V-8 and the fixed doublets tuh-duh/tuh-duh, tuh-duh/tuh-duh of cement-scored concrete highways, so perfectly rhythmic, as if driving on a road poem.

And me, so kid-happy, tucked up against the side window, staring at stars, as was my habit, through half-frosted, green-blued safety glass, dreaming kid dreams as was my entire job and purpose. Acutely aware of the radio skipping through the atmosphere, crackling and hissing, jumping over audio remnants of other stations, finally landing the strong signal of a late-night baritone voice, an audio oasis in the dark night. I remember my folks, silhouetted by the lovely mechanical glow of dashboard-and-radio light, sitting side-by-side as magnificent and steadfast guardians to my entire world. I can still feel the engine-warmed air of the front seat... sneaking one hand over the top, warming it up until it was just right, and then quickly drawing it back to the side of my cold cheek, and that was my first hint that heaven was a moment and not a place. And there was born my first conscious thought—that always we were going somewhere and that was just perfect for me, because somewhere was always where I wanted to be going.

Why does your old man love to travel, Little Ones? To be changed, and to be changed again and again. Because when you travel, really travel—getting deep down into the towns and people, the land and the culture—you will be forever changed. Changed into a person of the world. One who has completed the journey into tolerance and acceptance of the world's vagaries and differences. Changed to give a damn about everything and everybody, not just forever riding on the coattails of your own purpose-fully fenced and tightly mowed backyard of a world.

I love to travel, Little Ones, because of its essential curiosity. That endless bottomless human ache of inquisitiveness to explore what's ever around the next corner, over the next rise, or just beyond the horizon. It starts the moment you crawl, delving into every nook, investigating every cranny, until your baby body evolves into a miniature exploring machine. Then you are walking, which, like the explorers of old, puts you at the edges of your old map, now ready to make new. And unless you're taught how to be shackled and chained by society's (and your parents') definitions and deterrences, or to fall without question into all manner of sensibility and security, you will head out into the world with your will to explore and your curiosity intact. And that is what I wish, want, and desire so much for you both.

Sometimes I travel, Little Ones, just to be overwhelmed—for it's good every now and then to be overwhelmed. Because every now and then we just get to be too big for our britches and we need a little reducing. A little humbling just to be closer to the god and awe of it all. To be naturally and wonderfully diminished and purposefully overwhelmed. Trying to hunt down or stumble upon the divine proportion of life, that perfect imperfection which is nothing less than the confluence of God, nature, and man. And in travelling, we somehow find ourselves often closer to this grace and ideal.

Where did I learn to travel, Little Ones? In my mom and pa's living room, sitting numb-legged for hours at the altar of the bookshelf, where all the glorious maps and books were kept, awaiting their next convert.

It was the names, Little Ones. The names on those books, the names on those maps. Those gorgeous magical names that grind around your soul, like the enchanting magnitude of notes swirling around a grand cathedral—all that music trying to escape to heaven, trying to break through the thick walls and vaulted ceilings with all its earthly might. In the beginning, those names were persons—Roald Amundsen and the South Pole, Peary and the North. And the sailors, Magellan, Drake, Cook, Columbus, and Da Gama. Names you loved to say out loud. And our own boys, Lewis and Clark, on their wild trek across our new nation-in-the-making. Then there were the mysterious ones, Leif Ericson, Ibn Battuta, Marco Polo. Then the Brits with their insatiable wanderlust—Richard Burton and his Mecca, David Livingstone and his Africa.

And just when I thought I had reached the edge of my book-bound earth, I was then seduced, tantalized, heartsmitten, thunderstruck, maddened, and intoxicated with all the names on the maps, which like a madman's potion, drove your pa to desire Damascus, Paris, Nova Scotia, the Hebrides, the Dolomites, the Great Slave Lake, Gibraltar, Prague, Rome, Tangiers, any Alps, anything

New York, the Hindu Kush, Kilimanjaro, Denali, the Badlands, the Grand Canyon, Antarctica, the Seychelles, Burma, Mongolia and Ulan Bator, Russia and Moscow, Ayers Rock, the Himalayas, Angkor Wat, New Zealand, Easter Island, anywhere in the Amazon, the Gobi Desert, Oslo, Greenland, and any and all of every last fifty states in that grand playground known as America.

And then all that wonderful madness and desire was made real as the lit flame exploded into sun and I was granted entrance into my first and perfect moment of travel—the arriving, after days on the train, into evening Istanbul, an arriving from the new west into the old east, and suddenly like the child's picture book dream I had carried in my head for a thousand years, the kingdom appears like Cinderella and Ali Baba magic, my young man's face pushed up against the slowing breeze—and everywhere I am smelling the ancient spice of city and man and animal and existence, and hearing the age-incrusted antiquity of time captured and time still pulsing from the minarets, as the muezzins echo their sing-song human music to prayer—all this skin-prickly sensation of history living in and all around me, all this young-man symphony in a matter of a few minutes, now resounds in my memory, and will, until the day I end.

And it was at that perfect first moment of travel, I slowly began to understand one of the essential mysteries of travelling—the movement. The legs against the earth.

The lap of water against the ship. The slow and ancient cadence of a horse walking. The perfect and endless percussion of riding the rails. The purr/hum of rubber tire on road. That physical sensation of moving your body around the earth—and the eternal nomad of our past is again satisfied, not just to survive, but to be back home on the move.

I travel, Little Ones, not only for the passion and madness and desire of movement, but because travel, like bread and water and air, becomes necessary to a life fully dreamed and lived. It's through traveling you make the great journey into yourself, and it's the clarity of extremes in travelling that forces you to meet yourself like you've never met yourself before.

The great loneliness and solitude that are the secret passageways to travel's neverland are experienced as you lay fever-sick, shivering beyond control into the hollow of a small cluster of boulders, delirious to the night sky—lying on the wet fall ground in your sleeping bag, a stone's throw from the railway tracks, miles from humanity, waiting for the Corsican train that only arrives once a day. And your family and friends and god inside of you are the only medicine that can save you at that solitary and desolate moment.

And then, as capricious as a summer snowstorm, travel will grant you a great day of upending exaltations as you first meet the Pope while out for a sunrise stroll through St. Peter's Square, and then fifteen minutes afterwards, fall in love with an Italian goddess while you both drink from some ancient stone water fountain, your eyes meeting each other in that universal smile which is the language of love, lust, attraction, and sheer fright, and then somehow later that evening, across city and time and millions of Romans, you magically run into one another at the Trevi fountain (of all places), whereupon you assemble a whole host of strangers to act as your interpreter to ask her out on a date for that evening—and she accepts. And somehow you began to understand that travelling isn't just travelling...

Why do I travel, Little Ones? And the reasons seem infinite and simple and unfathomable, all at the same time. I travel to be replenished with beauty, for travel makes the beauty of this world seem like a Christmas that never ends. I travel for the jolting, angelic act of seeking strangeness and newness and profoundness. I travel because life is short, and I will not wait for fear of death or sanctuary to become a prison of my own making. I travel because I become uncomfortable being too comfortable. I travel for the sensation of changing into a magic costume as I enter some city or town in the dark starriness of night, to delight in the sorcery of waking up in a new land in the light of day. I travel because it makes me realize how much I haven't seen, how much I'm not going to see, and how much I still need to see. I travel for the great stories now ready to tell, and those waiting to be told. I travel to know where I fit into the world, and where I don't. I travel for the travelers I will meet; all of us drawn to the mystical chemistry of desiring movement and the electric fire of endless curiosity. Why do I travel, Little Ones...

Your mother and I loved to travel. Born to travel. Born to skip the cinders, as she was wont to say. Flying that newly-scrubbed Pontiac preening down back roads and blueroads, dirt roads and double-dotted roads, because hopes and promises were always waiting for us over the next rise. Drawing our fingers over the flat bible that was our road map—the gorgeous sensation of following the inked lines—knowing our bodies had traversed every mile of that road, and there was more road to feel. Shearing through space on the mechanical wings of a Saginaw transmission, and we both knew we were born again that very moment, with wind in our hair and all of our youth before us and all our curiosity quivering and gleaming in manic gypsy wanderlust, careening across and all over the big west and east of our country, brightening our souls like kids who had nothing but the biggest big backyard in all the world to explore.

I hope, Little Ones, that somewhere in all your genetic tomfoolery there is a gypsy strand that pulls you to the road. Gather up the maps to see if they sparkle for you. All the declinations and Mercator grids. All the contour lines and legends and scales. Every north and south, east and west. Every longitude and latitude whose meridians lead them back upon themselves. And all those delicious names just beckoning you to go to them. Go like your mom and your pa and become blessed and giddy as faithful gypsies. Go be changed, and awed, and everything. Go as a child, because to go a mile is going to the moon. Go to be scared, elated, and ever challenged. And always go because you are born to be curious, and you can never be curious enough—never.

And when you step out your door to go someplace, go for little reason and much rhyme, and because the going sounds much better than the staying, and because somehow it just tickles your fancy and sets your toes to tapping. And when you go with such a heart, then you will know you were made to travel, and happily and somehow I will know too.

Love,
Pa

Little Ones,

THE SANDMAN HAS YET TO KNOCK on my door again, but do I care? No—for now I have been given another song to entrust to you both. What a radiant gift to be granted tonight. I wonder how many more I will be given to write? I find it comforting, singing my words to you. And how well they seem to fit inside my wooden-walled universe. Like time inside a clock.

I believe myself into these songs, Little Ones. And by doing so, I become both song and singer right there before you. And with this bargain struck—for this momentary alignment of grace and music—I am allowed to stop all the minutes I want. All those ever anxious minutes so eagerly waiting to sweep me downstream to my ending.

These songs. Sometimes they arrive, as if from some strange and invisible middle in my room, appearing instantly out of nowhere, as if somehow slipping between gravity and memory, desperately wanting to be somewhere now.

And sometimes I feel as if I'm only a doorman awaiting the arrival of her royal majesty. Arriving without notice, she speaks with urgency, and immediately I am her amanuensis, scribbling down her every utterance as fast as my fingers will fly. When she is finished, she leaves as mysteriously and abruptly as she arrived, and I never know when she'll return.

My songs. They are my companions when I am lonely. The keeper of my secrets, even when I don't know what my secrets are. They are my devil's handshake between a good remembering and a sharp lamenting— and a divided liberation, giving me to both what is binding and painful, and what is an ecstasy and salvation.

Your old man was given a gift, Little Ones. To marry words and music together. And before, the only purpose for such a gift was to give it away. To unleash all those shiny notes, so eager to strut their giddiness before any audience they could find. To touch whomever, and for whatever reason. In amazement that this gift is still granted me, I now know its ultimate purpose—to be given to you, my children, my family. As both a legacy and a message. To vanquish time—to carry me straight into your hearts.

I wait for another song to arrive. There must be more music, for there is so little time. Of this I am certain.

Papa

10:20 p.m.

I REMEMBER YOU SITTING across from me at our kitchen table. Your wedding ring so silver-perfect around your finger.

It is evening, in winter. A hurly-burly snow is falling and a fire is burning hot in the cookstove. I smell fresh-baked bread and split pine. A poem lies within this perfect order of purpose and fulfillment, built into the true-ness of this house that protects. Now only small miracles are the order of the day. Somewhere there must be a dog for I hear a wheeze and a sigh near some table leg accompanied by a thrice-tailed whumping on a bare wooden floor. A dog dream, no doubt. A penny-whistle wind funnels through the cracks of some old and sun-warped window jamb and, like a winter feather, brushes up against my cheek, reminding me that outside all is chaotic but assured in the snowfall of God's domain.

Across this table, all mired in love and busyness and beauty, you configure and plot new destinies in wish-perfect dreams that are most innocently and absolutely out of my reach. I decide not to read another word to you tonight, for I haven't yet started, but choose to remain on this chair, next to this table, across from your gentle-hearted universe. Somehow I know that every goodness that could ever exist has fallen into my hands at this precise moment and that your every rain-sun smile and ballerina step and gracious word and Christmas kiss is now mine to treasure. And if ever grace visited a man in his dreams or in reality, then I feel I am blessed as the most fortunate man on earth. And this is how I sometimes think of you. Sitting across this table from me. As I wait for the dawn and the evening to mate again, in this snow-blessed and reverie night.

HOW DO YOU, my Little One, laugh in your sleep? You here, like a dream before me. Never knowing such a sensation. Nor the possibility.

But here you are laughing. Not out loud, but squirreling around inside your body like some private baby joke. Your little frame giggle-jiggles. Your chortle-red cheeks laugh-puffing in and out like a baby blowfish taken with himself. And yet you remain asleep, eyes closed, not caring a lick that the entire universe conspired to take a momentary breather from churning out galaxies and whipping up black holes, and conjured up this awe-gasping, wonder-working masterpiece before me of my Little One laughing in his sleep.

This little lamb of papa's who laughs. And now laughs again—your papa's heart bursting in a thousand bows to happiness as I gaze upon you like a prayer in the making. Now, I have seen heaven in my dying and dreaming. Here, in private miracle. And whether it is god or you, I don't care, because you are here, now, like angelsong and godspeed, sleeping and laughing within this house of my arms.

I'M ARRIVING HOME TO YOU.
From the darkness again, where I left you this
morning—

Moving hard against the brutish day where horse
and man, and trucks and men,
pounded the earth. And my body, bruised like a
boxer and damn dog-tired.

Now walking through the front door where the
stampede of little feet and
love-cooked dinner fills our home—this only
heaven possible.

And you both run into my arms, squealing the
only words that this man has waited
a day and a lifetime to hear—
"Papa."

TAKE OFF MY CLOTHES and there becomes a man. Take off my skin and there becomes my bones. Break all my bones and there becomes my heart. Smash my heart and there becomes my soul. And that you cannot take. And what is my soul? My family, my wife, my children, and my friends. It is my land, and the house and home that are built upon it. It is my honor and my name, my country and my God. It is my memory of what has made me. It is my hope for things that might be. It is my belief in what is right and what is wrong. It is my reason in times of self-deceit and my compassion in times of indifference. It is my gut and my intuition. It is everything that makes me foolhardy, brave, unkind, or steadfast. It is my mystery given to me to never solve. It is everything that makes a man. It is everything that makes this man.

And that is who I am alive, and that is who I am dead.

December 4

Little Ones,

NOW IT IS SUNSET. On this day and at this hour, your mother and I were married. We stood on the ridge that overlooks the ranch, next to the cottonwood cross and amidst our family and friends. Even Boots and Grace, whom we rode in on, stayed close at hand during the ceremony. Your mom recited the vows from memory, as if she had always known them by heart. Your pa, suddenly realizing the magnificence of the moment, stopped in midsentence, catching himself up on the godliness of the twilight-blue sky, the horses grazing nearby, and the profound beauty of your mother. That moment will be my last dream.

Little Ones, I give to you our vows—that which your mother and I wrote so many lifetimes ago. I hope you look upon our promise not as the inevitability of two lives now seemingly undone but as the deep devotion of two people who once believed—still believe—in the great possibilities of an enduring love.

Papa

I take you to be my wife:
And here under God's eyes, upon this powerful and sacred earth which brought us together, before the clan

of our families and the loyalty of our friends, we will now begin a new journey, bound only in covenant by the hand of Providence and the truth and courage of our hearts revealed.

My vow to you is thus:

I promise from this day forward to love you as my wife, my lover, my protector and friend. To stand by you in all of life's precariousness and abundance—in sickness and in health, in plenty and in want. And when you are in harm's way, I will defend you with my life. I promise to dream with you both great dreams and small dreams. To ask your counsel in times of uncertainty. To honor your silence when you seek to be alone. To be ever wondrous at your curiosities and revelations. And to be ever rejuvenated by your passions.

I will strive valiantly with you in all endeavors and worthy causes of the soul. And when you fall, I shall give you my strength to stand again. And when you are glorious, together we will remember the sacrifices given and we will be humbled. Now I seek life with you, and only you. To laugh with you in joy; to grieve with you in sorrow; to grow with you in love; till death do us part.

This is my vow to you.

Now I take you to be my husband…

December 7
clear and cold

The Church of Earth and Sky

Little Ones,

T HERE IS A CHURCH I go to.
I walk to this church in the rain.
I walk to this church in the snow.

Although I am not a man of a formal God, one who arrives with many rules and smoke and exhortation, I still go to this most magnificent church.

Its walls are many: the pine and piñon trees; the arroyos and canyons; the green shale mountain and the shearing granite cliffs.

Its ceiling is the Pleiades and Orion. And a thousand more stars whose names I cannot remember. Its grand chandelier is an incandescent harvest moon. And when the night church is finished building itself, then it gives way to the day church. Its candelabra becomes the slow solstice sun as it meanders up the ridgeline and beyond. And the vaulted beams of its ceiling are now the reddening grey thunderclouds of a new storm unveiling.

I go to this church where a Chinook wind comes to calm my heavy soul.

I go to this church for a mid-autumn's rain to wash away the tears of a sorrowing heart.

I go to this church to feel a colding winter that silences my confusion and fear with the feathered grace of a million falling snow crystals.

I go to this church where the sermons of earth and sky teach me once again of where I was born and what I must follow.

I go to this church that gives no judgment or damnation. It is always a beginning, always a deep silence, and forever the primal.

It is a desolate church. It is built in the sundowns and horizons of what is vast and trembling in the universe.

It does not need a preacher.

It does not need a bible.

What is taught here is given only to those who listen. Given in quiet words and in ways not obvious. It is both forgiving and unrelenting. With no guilt or apology. And every day sees a sacrifice and a hope.

And who cannot wonder at the maker of such a church?

At such beauty and harshness?

Yet, for all its wildness and mystery it is a most honest church, and I would have no other.

I go to this church in these, my darkest moments. Where sometimes a bitter cold wind strikes my cheeks and ears. Where sometimes a blackness of sky and a torrent of rain drown my head and body. Where sometimes the most quieting silence to my mind occurs between the howl of the coyote and the cutting swoosh of a crow's wings against the snow- air. This is my communion. This is my final blessing. In the hollow within me of that which is unknowing and mournful, I am given to this grace of the rain and the howl, and the wind and the snow, and I am calmed.

night

I REMEMBER so much now…

Singing to you with my guitar while you bathed in the ocean of the claw-foot tub—sitting on the bench outside the small open window, hearing the muffled water splashes echoing off the walls. Playing most every song I'd ever written and knowing you were listening.

Your hiding the small bronze horse in my saddle bag for luck. Or in my suitcase when I was on the road. I forgot how that history got started. Small notes tucked into my pants pocket or into my wallet. Elfin epistles that appraised the universe and sprinkled true Juliets everywhere, reminding me of who and what was truly important.

The way you danced. You loved to dance. A body that craved dance more than food or water. Like wick and candle—whose only reason to exist is to be on fire. Peering around the corner of the living room, watching you dance to the music in your head. Crazy over your magic. Always wondering how you were made.

How you welcomed me home. Every evening. Like

it was a bona-fide homecoming parade. Like Billy Yank coming home from the war—to see his gal still standing up on the balcony—to be garlanded and hugged, then covered in squeals of anticipation.

I remember watching you plant the garden behind the barn, fending off the sun with that big, sun-beaten straw hat that Mankey got down in Mexico and gave to you, ministrating to squash and tomatoes, roses and herbs. Lost in your work like a little prairie girl building earth prayers. Happy. As in a perfect and pure happiness. The kind that God gives you, which you never really know how to use. But I learned how from you.

Your painting watercolors, trying to speak Spanish, plunking out some new tune on the upright. Fingers splayed over needlework or some mysterious project, surrounded by a moat of pencils and paint, cloth and paper, stardust and velveteen.

I remember getting up to stoke the fire, bringing you your morning cup of servant-served, Cleopatra-and-cowboy coffee. While embers crickered in the morning darkness and snow whisperfell against the window glass.

Your reading our old love letters. Sometimes our loud. And why should I have been embarrassed, and yet

I was. Embarrassed as men get at such romantic keep-sakery, but somewhere inside I was secretly pleased. Wondering now what will become of them. Are they for others to find?

My arm blanketing you in the middle of the night. Listening to winter wind outside the open window. Dog-tucked beneath our warm covers—where at the edge of our quilted universe lay our room, deliciously cold. Taking comfort in the smell of your hair, watching you breathe in baby's sighs. To want you by my side again.

I wonder what it would be like to hold you now. How would you feel?

I wonder who you are with now. If he touches you as I do.

Will you listen again to the songs I gave you? Where I reached for the guitar in dead-of-night darkness, trying to catch the just-dreamt lyric or string of notes—like try-ing to snatch an angel's echo.

And I really wonder if these words will ever find you—or you them?

I remember once kissing you, your face lit by north-ern stars. Promising to grow old with you, and now so simply breaking the promise. Do you remember?

Reading now my half of our wedding rings—
"nothing is impossible." And does yours still exists?
—"for valiant hearts."

Racing toward the edge of my universe, am I still
within you?

Dec. 15

YEARS AGO, in another lifetime, I carved these words on my guitar. They are on the backside, beneath the mountains. So powerful, calming this troubled head of mine more times than I can remember. It is good to know that such Bible words of beauty and strength exist to this very clock and hour:

"But they that wait upon the Lord shall renew their strength; they shall mount up with wings as eagles; they shall run, and not be weary; and they shall walk, and not faint."

December 24
snow-cold clear

Little Ones,

I AM WITH YOU NOW. On this last and beautiful
Christmas...

Teaching you how to build glorious snowmen that
would stand all around the house like loyal soldiers.

Riding through the snowdrift morning on steaming
horses far up into the woods to consider, and scrutinize,
and then discover the perfect Christmas tree.

Stringing long necklaces of popcorn and cranberries
together to later hang upon the tree—just as my brothers
and I did when we were kids.

Now hauling out, with your mother's help, the Yule
log that's been drying for the last year in the back of the
barn, and laying it on the firedogs.

Like little electric poems—as every day you count
and then discover yet another Christmas present with
your name on it beneath the tree.

As I smoke my pipe and drink some wonderful Viking Christmas concoction that your Mom once dreamed up, the air filled with Jerusalem scents, all of us gather at the sacred and appointed hour to put the decorations on the tree.

Listening to your mom explain to you in impeccable kid logic that to make it snow on Christmas eve you should wear your pajamas inside out and backwards—and get as many of your friends as possible to do the same.

With your Christmas-Day-will-never-arrive-soon-enough salivations, you anticipate the moment when, like voracious cub lions, you'll rip open the wrapping paper and feast off your every delicious present.

Laying out, for Santa's midnight visit, a fulsome plate of chocolate-chip cookies, angel wings, and milk—and, just for good measure (following your pa's advice), three hanks of smoked beef jerky and some of Grandpa's best Yule bourbon (usually only half a bottle). And in the morning, as my folks did in Norman Rockwell secrecy, watching you run to the plate like detectives to a crime to see how hungry Santa truly was.

Walking outside in the crunching snow and Christmas-Eve cold to give the horses and the dogs their special dinners.

You both finally falling asleep in manger innocence, like little baby Jesuses. Perfect in this moment. And time does stop.

While all the universe and my family are still sleeping, I will walk among the red and blue twinkle-lights of the living room, to sit and gaze upon the pretty white angel atop the tree and say silent prayers, remembering what was good in the world and why I was brought here to remember.

Dec. 26
night and clear

How utterly, utterly small we are under this magnificent star canopy. My God, what a sensation to be an atom in the scheme of such grandiosity. The allurement, the jazz, and the physics of it all. And how well love reigns under and over this convergence of infinity, all, and everything. My God, what wonders we must behold before we go. To be awakened. And so awake.

Little Ones,

D REAM LIKE YOUR OLD MAN...

Dreams are about anticipation. Dreams are about hope. When you're a kid, you need to trust your dreaming. It's not about asking for the moon. It's about going to the moon. About choosing to explode into possibility. It's about your chewing every night and every day on a piece of the future.

Dreams are about secret secrets and wishbook desires. The hither and hilly of wanting and expectation. The unknown guiding the known. The Daniel Boone of it all. Always wanting more elbow room whenever smoke is seen on the horizon.

Dreams are about tilting your head up toward the desert sky where stars are dazzling in hot and white, and the autumn is snapping cold on the nape of your neck. Dreams are about the Milky Way mantling across the universe like some saucy necktie, all temptation and God and wonder rolled into one. And as you look up, you think you're the first person ever to notice how magnificent the heavens really are. And you dream as a pioneer dreams, of stout homes and greener valleys. This is how your old man looks at the world. This is how I dream.

And even though I know each dream is given to me in a silver moment and could be taken away from me in a titanic flip of the wrist, upending a card game that some peevish gods didn't care to play anymore, all that's left in the end is to persevere. To go on and on, and forward and on, and never ever stop. Is your old man making sense?

Dream bravely. Forget the gods and face your fears. Don't let little terrors hobble you like a bunch of gremlins manacled to your ankles, constantly nipping and biting at you. Find fearlessness inside of you. Dare, and fear will falter. Challenge, and fear will flee. This is the beginning to your dream-making.

Become the dream-farer. You are only here now, and then you are gone. So be hungry. Hunger toward beauty. Hunger toward love. Hunger toward the unimaginable and unthinkable. Be bulldogged and tigerish toward your dream. Bite off Jupiter and then ask for Saturn. And fall. Fall hard. Tumble to the ground earth-headfirst. Pick yourself up again and again, brush off the dirt and the dirt roads, and push yourself through walls and walk through fires just for the hell of it, and all reasons and none.

Do not give a damn what "they" have to say (and you will know who they are) for you are either very right or very wrong, but at least you are very something. You can live with this firefaith. However mighty or small, it is the heartbeat that emboldens you to dream. Be fiery with your life and all your dreaming. If you fear, eat the fear. If you die, taste the tears upon your tongue. If you die, then die well and with dignity, knowing that you've left few stones unturned and no love unrequited.

Every day can be your deathbed—your exacting. So dream in storms, and dream in revelation. Do so honestly to who you are, what you want to be, where you want to go, and whom you want to love. You are given this bull's-eye, crackerjack choice every twenty-four hours of your existence. And as I once saw written on a barroom wall: "No eternal reward will forgive us now for wasting the dawn of today."

What do I say now? You are being born into a savage, frenzied, and uproarious world, and I cannot be there for you. Nor can I shield you from misfortune and sorrow. It is you who must someday break through the protective polish of who you are, to become naked and powerful to who you can truly be. You who must learn of God and mortality, of surrender and fight, of image and substance. Your destiny will lie between all these truths.

So begin now. Move fast and furiously toward your destiny. All galloping body and heaving lungs, all aching to break free. Dash yourself forward into the arms of destiny, laden with dreams and drunk with hope. For destiny needs you to dream. It has no other purpose.

Dream with intention. Like the poet-king and song-queen who must both create and protect their dreams. Pour yourself into the molten metal of your own forge. Become solid and strong. Then be like a juggernaut that has no brakes.

Dream young. Don't settle for old—for to be old is to be superstitious and without curiosity and always questioning faith. And be ferocious in your dreaming—run like a sun's explosion, and skip across bluing waves, and dance upon tips of swan feathers.

Dream. Dream like a circus. Colorful—like clowns begging to be tilted sideways just to make you do the same—and you forever wanting more, like rolling down a hill until you're spinning with the world, sick like a joke and bursting into laughter, and then you run to the top of the hill to start all over again. And everywhere there is that boisterous and seductive calliope, bellowing and orating, making melodic fancy and fortune—and suddenly you clutch your papa by the hand as you look in true belief and disbelief at the man flying through the air, hurtling himself over gravity and slack-jawed malcontents, and you hope that he just keeps on flying right through the roof and on and on because that would be the cat's pajamas and the best cotton candy and the greatest magic on earth which it should be and is.

Dream.

Dream like a painting.

Dream like an opera.

Dream like the horse and rider.

Dream like the prince and princess.

Dream like the circus.

Dream with god-fire and planet-glory, and don't worry that they won't last forever because they won't and they will, and I know this—and now you hear this—and always you must know it in your belly, deep within your gut and heart—the engines behind your soul.

I love you both.

Dream always with love.

And dream with passion.

Dream for yourself and to the world.

Dream to the stars and to more stars and to all and every damn star in the whole Big Banging, grandiloquential, damn-fool mass and maze of desire and never-ending chance and fate that operates under the guise known as the universe. It's all yours, my darlings.

Now Dream.

Papa

Dec. 31.

T O REMEMBER YOU so vividly, dancing there, with sweet champagne pulsing through your veins... to know what it's like to feel another's presence pulsing through mine. And each time, looking forward to popping that enchanted cork with you and really disappearing from the world as we knew it—wondering if we would ever return.

I WONDER WHAT YOU two are doing right now?

My imagination is endless…

Night

My Love,

WILL YOU remember?

Past fences that must fall,
toward valleys that will yield.
Upon horses daring,
under nightfall's luscious moon.
Where glances are met and
touches conceived,
as onward we go,
never once looking back.

I LOVE YOU both. My God, how much I love you. Be
brave now. I will be with you always.

Standing at the edge of this forever, I see geom-
etries of stars and infinities and godliness I have never
seen before. Here I must begin again.

I love you, Little Ones.

I love you, my Darling.

I am with you. Always.

It is time now. I must go.

*Is the **Journey** over?*

Or has it just begun?

If You Could . . .

LIVE

all the days and nights of the father's last seven months, of his race to finish his letters for his wife and children . . .

DISCOVER

all the stories and wisdom-giving that become his children's "guidebook to life" . . .

EMBRACE

all the desire, struggle, and ultimately the redemption of the great love between him and his wife . . .

FEEL

all his great joys—and his immense desolation, his inspiring and poignant memories, his powerful, relentless, yearning to live . . .

Would You Wish for More?

Now Read

All the timeless and universal letters

from their very beginning

to their incredible ending . . .

<u>in</u>

The Legacy Letters ∾ Complete ∾

And now, for the first time,

listen to the haunting and beautiful

♪ *"gift of songs"* ♪

the father also gave to his family

The Legacy Letters—Complete
The Legacy Letters—The Songs

Available <u>Now</u> at

www. The LegacyLetters.com

A Lifetime Lived in

7 Months

12 Songs

& 200 Letters

www. TheLegacyLetters.com

"Dream like your Old Man…"

"I wake up. The moon is still out."

Once upon a time your papa wrote and played music

"Morning. Cut out in vast blocks
of green and blue."

Musical Mountains
and the Cabin

"Your voice inside my head… Fireworks Memory…"

Take off my clothes and there
becomes a man.

How utterly, utterly small we are under this magnificent star

"I want to have so many memories of you."

There Are Hard Days to Live

A Most Important Letter

**Toast Your Old Man and
Remember the Seasons**

"I remember so mu

How do you, my Little One, laugh in your s

To remember you so vividly, d

"I am with you now. On

The Art of Work and

Who w

"I spy a mermaid-green I have neve

Your Old Man's Dec

The Everyth

Plea

My Tw

Congratulations